A TIME TO
KILL,
A TIME TO DIE

CHARLES RAY

North Potomac, MD

This book is a work of fiction. Names, descriptions, places, and incidents are products of the author's imagination, or are used fictionally. Any resemblance to actual events or persons, living or dead, is purely coincidental.

The reproduction or distribution, by any means, including electronic distribution, is expressly prohibited without the written consent of the copyright holder, except for fair use quotes in connection with reviews.

For information about this and other works of this author, contact the author at charlesray.author@yahoo.com.

Printed in the United States of America.

Dedication

It's common on a dedication page to thank everyone who contributed in any way to the creation of a book. For this, and my other works, such a list would be far too long, for I've been inspired and helped along the way by so many people. So, I'll just say thanks to everyone who believed in me, when there were times I wasn't sure that I believed in myself, to everyone who held out a hand when I needed to be pulled out of the doldrums. You know who you are, for you're the type person who does this for everyone. I would also like to dedicate this book to those few readers who keep coming back to read my feeble attempts at storytelling, who give me comments from time to time on what works, and, more importantly, what doesn't. You are why I do this. You, the reader, are why any writer sits down day after day, pounding out word after word, page after page. I hope you will find something to like about this book, and if you do, that you'll take the time to write a review—no matter how short—because, reviews draw attention to books, attract new readers, and that's what we writers are all about, getting more people to read what we write.

ONE

The sizzling sound of four strips of bacon turning brown in the skillet competed with the muted sound of water rushing through old pipes. The sweet aroma of maple-cured pork wafting up from the big iron skillet was tempting, but it lost out to the mental image of Sandra, fresh from the shower, her luscious body smelling of lilac from her soap. The thought of her standing under the shower head with the water cascading over her athletic form, caressing every curve, nook, and cranny, body-checked my attention and shoved it away from the bacon for a few seconds, almost long enough for it to burn. Fortunately, I'd done my meditation after taking my own shower, so I was able to slide the images of her into one part of my brain, while another concentrated on the breakfast I was preparing for the woman who was at that moment using up what was left of the hot water.

Sandra Winter, teacher at Carter High School in the District of Columbia's Southwest section, was the reason the water pipes were making noise. I met her several years ago during my investigation into the death of one of her students. Our initial encounter was rocky—I'd actually suspected her of killing the kid at one point—but, once we got to know each other, she'd helped me come out of the self-imposed isolation I'd been in since my wife, Sarah, and my almost six-year-old son, Ethan, had been killed when a truck driver had run a signal and T-boned the mini-van Sarah was driving. She and Ethan had been killed instantly along with most of the members of Ethan's soccer team. They'd been playing an evening game against a team in Arlington, Virginia, and were on their way back into the District around seven in the evening, neither too late nor too dark, with the northbound traffic on Arlington Boulevard light, and no reason for the son of a bitch to do what he did other than he'd been drinking and he was in a hurry. He wasn't even scratched, but the mini-van had been a twisted, almost unrecognizable wreck. Everyone inside had died, and when Detective Buster Mayweather, accompanied by two uniforms—one from DC Metro Police and one from Arlington County—had come to our brownstone house in the Georgetown area to deliver the sad news, a piece of me died as well.

But, I digress. I met Sandra almost ten years after the accident. Ten years during which time I'd lived mostly alone. I'd been in the army at the time of the accident, assigned to a desk job at the Pentagon; one of hundreds of lieutenant colonels working in what we often dubbed 'the five-sided Puzzle Palace.' I had my twenty in, and wasn't likely to be promoted to colonel. I'd been dissatisfied with my career for some time, and their deaths just completed a process that had been ongoing, so I put in my papers and retired.

I pretty much turned into a hermit for the first few weeks until one of the few friends I had—and, still have—Quincy Chang, partner in a DC law firm—talked me into using the skills I'd learned in the army. With his insistence, I did what was necessary to get my private investigation license, including doing a stint with one of the established firms in the city to accumulate the required number of hours, and opened a one person firm in a seedy building off Fourth Street in Southwest DC not far from Fort McNair, the historic old army post where the Lincoln assassination conspirators had been hung. After less than a week, I'd realized that while I could do the investigation part with no problem, keeping the books just wasn't my thing. I put an ad in the *Washington Post* for a secretary/bookkeeper. Heather Bunche, who had just that week graduated from secretarial school, and in need of a job as much as I was in need of help, was the first applicant. I knew nothing about hiring a secretary. She was impressive, though. All five feet, two inches of her, with her light blonde hair pulled back into a no-nonsense ponytail, so I hired her. Turned out to be the best decision I ever made. An organized person, she was a great secretary, she knew enough math to make sure our books balanced at the end of each month, and more importantly, she was a Houdini with computers and information retrieval. After ten years, I made her a full partner after helping her get her license.

These are just about the only people in my life now, at least, the only ones I call friend. Buster Mayweather, now a detective lieutenant in DC Metro's homicide bureau—along with his petite wife, Alma, and their twins Albert and

Sandra, which is another story entirely; Quincy Chang, who I've known since we met at Fort Bragg, North Carolina, when he was in the JAG office there and I was assigned to the Special Warfare Center; Heather Bunche, my partner; and, of course, Sandra Winter, who I guess you would call my girlfriend.

Sandra owns a small house in Takoma Park, a middle class enclave of small single family houses and turn of the century townhouses in the District's Northwest, but for a couple of years she'd stayed at my place more or less full time, only going back to her house to check that it hadn't been broken into or that a water pipe hadn't burst. I've suggested a time or two that she should rent it out, but she resists. Sometimes I wonder if she's worried that our relationship won't last. Hell, it's been almost ten years now. Not, mind you, that I'm one to talk. I'm pretty set in my own ways.

My mind came back to the bacon, which was now perfectly done on both sides. Nice and golden brown, with only narrow strips of white fat. I took the slices out and laid them out precisely atop a square of paper from the large roll on the counter next to the sink to allow the remaining grease to leach out, leaving them crisp like we liked them.

I then walked to the refrigerator, a large side-by-side fridge/freezer combination, and removed two eggs, a block of cheddar, some fresh green onions, a couple of ripe jalapeño peppers, and a clove of garlic. I broke the eggs into one bowl, whipping them until they were a light yellow and frothy, and chopped, shredded, or diced the rest of the ingredients into another. I put a teaspoon of salt, two teaspoons of black pepper, and a dash of cumin into the egg mixture and beat it some more. After draining most of the bacon grease from the skillet, I put it back on the stove over medium heat and watched until I saw small waves of vapor undulating up from its black iron bottom. I poured the egg mixture in. It immediately began solidifying around the edges and bubbling in the middle. I waited a few seconds, and then dumped in the dry ingredients, sprinkled tabasco sauce liberally over everything, and then folded the nearly circular egg in half, holding the top down until the two halves were sealed together. After a minute, I flipped it over, and let it cook for another minute. I then slid it out of the skillet and onto a large platter.

I was thinking about doing a pan of biscuits, but I noticed that the sound of water through the pipes had stopped. Sandra would be in the kitchen shortly, and after our morning exercise would be as hungry as I was, and in no mood to wait for biscuits to cook. So, I put two slices of bread in the toaster, and two more on a saucer near the toaster.

With the cooking just about done and her shower over, the place was quiet. We live in an old farm house off River Road in Montgomery County, Maryland, a few miles west of the little village of Potomac; home to many of the area's rich and famous. I'd bought it at an estate sale a few months after Sarah and Ethan's funeral, wanting out of the neighborhood we'd lived in for three years, and the pitying looks and attempts to be consoling from the people there, who had known the two of them, but who had barely spoken two words to me when they were alive. The place was a two-story square with porches front and rear, and a fireplace in the living room. Upstairs was a master bedroom and two smaller bedrooms, each with its own bath. Downstairs I had a living room, a somewhat smaller dining room, and the kitchen. Pretty simple, and more than adequate for my needs. The place had been solidly built in the 1920s, so the only thing I'd done was upgrade the kitchen with all-new appliances, and put in heavier front and back doors. A barn sat behind the house, between the house and the forest that stretched westward and downhill toward the C&O Canal and the Potomac River. In winter, we often parked our cars in the barn, which was more than large enough, and wasn't used for anything else but a place to keep my heavy kicking bag and for martial arts practice.

With the forest behind and on two sides, and River Road—sparsely traveled except during morning and evening rush hour—a quarter mile to the east, there is little but the sound of nature. You can get used to the chirping of birds and insects. The house, though, is solidly built like I said, and nature's sounds don't penetrate that much. Makes it nice for listening to music on the radio, which is my main form of entertainment. I don't own a television. Sandra complained at first, but after a while, didn't miss it. Turned out, there was nothing on TV that had ever struck her fancy anyway. So, we both got our entertainment and news by listening to the local National Public Radio station. I had a radio in the kitchen, and one in the living room. I reached across the sink and turned it on, just in time to hear the English accent of the morning news announcer, ". . . *Waylon was pronounced dead at 12:08 Eastern Standard Time by the prison doctor. Again, Henry Waylon, convicted of the rape and murder of Colleen Adamson in 1992, spent the last ten years at Sussex State Prison in Waverly, Virginia. He was moved to Greenville Correctional Facility in Jarratt a week ago. He was executed by lethal injection last night after Virginia's governor refused to grant a stay applied for by the condemned man's lawyer. Waylon went to his death proclaiming his innocence. That's the morning's news. Stay tuned for 'All Things Considered,' followed by a presentation of the Boston Philharmonic."*

"Ooh, that's terrible," Sandra's voice, behind and to the right, was tense.

"Yeah, I was kinda hoping for Mozart," I said.

"Not that," she said. "I mean the execution of Henry Waylon."

"Oh, that. Well, I'm no supporter of capital punishment, but he *was* found guilty of a pretty gruesome crime."

Not, I thought to myself, that killing him would bring the dead girl back, and the statistics on murder, or even rape for that matter, demonstrated that the death penalty didn't serve as a deterrent.

"But, don't you think his protesting his innocence right up until the moment they put the tubes in his arm indicate that he might have been wrongfully convicted?"

The stricken look on her face, and the glisten of unshed tears in her eyes told me that she'd been powerfully affected by the news. Just one more reason I didn't particularly care for network news reports and the way they flogged stories like this for all they were worth. NPR doesn't usually go in for that type of journalism, but I guess even they felt they had to cover this story.

I began moving the food to the little square

table in the breakfast nook just off the kitchen, hoping the delicious aroma of bacon and western omelet would take her mind off the story. If that didn't work, I was hoping the cup of freshly brewed Colombian coffee would do the trick.

It didn't at first. She picked at the omelet and only nibbled at the toast. She brightened up a little after taking a bite from a crispy strip of bacon, but her face really lit up after taking a sip of rich, dark coffee. I thought I'd gotten her mind out of the doldrums.

"You like the coffee?" I asked.

"I certainly do," she said. "The rest of the breakfast's not half bad either."

I beamed. Hell, I like getting compliments as much as the next guy. "Thanks. Anything to please my favorite lady."

She blew me a kiss. The rest of the meal went quietly and peacefully. When we'd finished, she helped me clear the table, and was quiet as we washed the dishes. It was only when the last plate was dried and stacked in the cabinet that she turned to me with a sad look in her blue eyes.

"There's a rumor that the defense asked for a DNA analysis of the evidence found at the crime scene," she said. "And, they were pretty confident the results would exonerate their client."

I shrugged. I was pretty sure it wasn't the first time an innocent person was put to death. Despite the long time allowed for appeals, I got a sense that most people, especially those who lived in states that still had the death penalty, just didn't give a damn. They were unable to identify with the occupants of death's row, most of whom were minorities, and besides, it was someone else's problem.

"That would be sad," I said.

"Is that all you can say? It would be sad?"

I could have said more, but it would only have started an argument, and I didn't feel like arguing, so I just shrugged again. I had a feeling that my day would only go downhill from there.

TWO

After the kitchen was back to its normal spotless condition, I got myself ready for work.

Since hanging up my army uniform, I've mostly wear casual clothing for work. Not jeans, but wash-and-wear pants, khaki or heavy-duty cotton, mostly brown or blue, with matching shirts. In winter I tend to long-sleeved shirts with a jacket to keep out the cold, but in July, with the heat and humidity in Washington, I stick mostly to short sleeves. If I have to meet someone important, I throw on a light jacket. I have five or six ties, mostly red or blue, but only wear those three or four times a year— for funerals or other formal occasions.

I checked my shirt, a tan one, to make sure the collar was straight. No sense looking scruffy. I then took my light brown jacket off the rack and draped it over my arm.

Sandra was sitting on the sofa in the living room flipping through a *Good Housekeeping* magazine when I came down.

"What are your plans for the day, babe," I asked.

She folded over the page she'd been reading, put the magazine on the cushion next to her beautifully curved hip, and looked up at me.

She smiled, but her eyes still looked sad.

"I think I'll go over to Montgomery Mall around mid-morning," she said. "The crowds shouldn't be too bad on Wednesday. You know we have that barbecue at Buster's this weekend, so I thought I'd pick up some gifts for the twins."

School had been out since early June, and she'd had nothing to do for six weeks except for the weekend activities and the occasional night out. Thankfully, my caseload had been light, so I'd been able to get home before six each day to keep her company. Teaching a bunch of inner city high school students kept her hopping during the school year, but she liked being active. She'd been dropping hints about maybe the two of us taking a trip around mid-August, and I was hoping things would stay quiet so that we'd be able to do it.

"While you're out, why don't you drop by a travel agency and see what kinds of trips are available for next month," I said.

Her eyes brightened, and her smile widened.

"That's a great idea. You have any special place you'd like to go?"

I thought about it for a few seconds. Actually, there was a trip I'd wanted to take for years, but had never gotten around to. A vacation that I was sure we'd both like.

"I've always wanted to visit Yellowstone Park, and maybe see the Black Hills. It might be a bit crowded, being the end of summer and all, but maybe we could go camping, just the two of us and Mother Nature."

Her expression became skeptical.

"That would be a long drive," she said. "You know how you hate long road trips. Sure you're up to it?"

That was for sure. My Volkswagen was too small for such a long trip, and her little Honda wasn't much better.

"I was thinking we could fly out and rent an RV and some camping gear."

I could see the wheels turning in her head. The skepticism was fading.

"You've been giving this some thought, haven't you?"

"Sure I have," I said. "We both deserve some time away from the grime of this city, and I've always wanted to see that part of the country."

"Okay then, I'll check out some trip packages."

She rose from the sofa and threw her arms around my neck, and kissed me on the cheek. She was back to her normal, ebullient self.

"Great," I said. "And, don't forget, we're going out for Korean food tonight."

She rubbed her pelvis against my thigh, and pulled my head down to plant her warm lips against mine. The news story before breakfast was forgotten—or, so I hoped.

I hadn't forgotten it, though. It was there in the middle part of my mind, like an itch that you can't quite reach. I'm like that. Sometimes things just lodge themselves in my mind and hang around like gnats buzzing your head at a picnic.

By the time I pulled my green Volkswagen— The Bug—onto River Road and pointed it south toward the I-495 Beltway, most of my mind was diverted to the traffic. Out where we live, the traffic is light, but within a mile, with all the morning commuters coming onto River Road from the winding streets that snake out of the trees on both sides, it starts to get heavy. The buzzing of the news story faded. I had to keep an eye out for the Mercedes and BMWs that often pulled out in front of me without slowing down or looking, or the dolts in front of me who were reading their papers as they drove, and who often slowed down to look more closely at what they were reading, mindless to the fact that they posed a hazard to everyone else on the road.

The traffic got really heavy and chaotic by the time I got to the turnoff to the Beltway, complicated by cars exiting River Road to the Beltway itself, and those taking the exit from the Beltway or River Road, but wanting to cross over and get onto Cabin John Parkway, which was my intent. I narrowly avoided being sideswiped by a big blue pickup that waited until the very last moment to slide over onto the ramp leading up to I-495, but managed to finally get onto the curving route that's Cabin John Parkway. All of this, mind you, takes place at speeds varying from 45 to 60 and higher. With a sigh of relief, I settled back for a less hectic ride on the parkway as it wound between grass and tree-covered hills toward Clara Barton Parkway and eventually Canal Road, which, while heavily traveled, is at sane speeds due to the patrolling of the U.S. Park Police who have jurisdiction over all lands and roads within national parks, and the area from Clara Barton Parkway in Montgomery County, Maryland into the District of Columbia is one big national park.

From Chain Bridge, which spans both the C&O Canal and the Potomac River, Canal Road is one way south in the morning and one way north in the evening, so there's no worry about head-on collisions. You still have to watch for the occasional unthinking motorist who slows

down without warning, but it's otherwise a
scenic drive. Not as beautiful as the George
Washington Memorial Parkway that runs
parallel on the Virginia side of the Potomac, but
a close second, with honeysuckle covered hills
to the east and a view of the canal and
occasionally the river to the west.

Canal Road intersects with Foxhall and
merges into M Street just below the stadium at
Georgetown University. I stayed in the right line
as I came off Canal and turned onto Whitehurst
Freeway, an elevated highway that runs along
what was once the docks and warehouse
district of Georgetown, with the Georgetown
Channel, where the Georgetown rowing team
practices, on my right. I got off Whitehurst and
onto Twenty-Sixth Street, driving south until I
could merge with the traffic on the Rock Creek-
Potomac Parkway, which swings behind Lincoln
Memorial. Past the memorial, I turned west on
Independence Avenue, then south on Maine
Avenue, west on M Street and then south on
Fourth Street, and drove the remaining three
blocks to my office in Southwest District.

On Maine Avenue, as it runs south under
the I-395 Expressway, you can see the changes
that are taking place in the city outside the Mall
and government area to the north. Once a
mainly working class and poor area, with little
two story townhouses surrounded by postage-
stamp sized, garbage strewn yards, it is now a
forest of high-rise condos and construction
cranes. The poor who once inhabited the area
are being squeezed south toward the Anacostia
River.

The building housing A.E. Pennyback,
Confidential Enquiries, though, is still a relic
from the pre-gentrification days. A two-story,

shoebox-shaped building with a porch running across the front of the second floor, it looked like those old motels you see along back roads in the south. There were six rooms on each floor, each housing a different small business. There was a bail bondsman on the ground floor, and a tax accountant upstairs where Heather and I hung out. I didn't know much about the other outfits. I'd only met the bail bondsman and the tax accountant when we all three arrived in the parking lot in front of the building at the same time one blistery winter morning and the two of them introduced themselves.

Our office was on the second floor, near the middle. I could reach it by way of either of the stairs at the ends of the porch, and since our assigned parking spaces were near the center, it hardly mattered which one I took.

The lot was full at 7:50 when I pulled in and parked next to Heather's blue Datsun.

She was sitting at her desk staring at her laptop when I walked in. It wasn't unusual for her to be at her desk at her computer—she almost always beat me in and was still there when I left—but, it the look on her face *was* unusual.

Heather Bunche, a five-two, well proportioned, pixie-like blonde, could be the poster girl for good cheer. She was usually smiling, and had a way of finding the positive side of most situations. Now, though, she was looking at her computer as if it was a cockroach and she wanted to smash it.

"What's up, Honeybunch," I said, using the nickname that I was the only person on earth she allowed to use.

When she looked up at me, I could see the streaks of tears on her cherubic cheeks, and the whites around the bright blue circles of her pupils were reddish. Her lips trembled, and then she pointed at the screen of her computer.

I walked over to see what she was pointing at. It was a reproduction of a news article that had appeared in a small newspaper that I'd never heard of:

Breaking News!
DNA Indicates Condemned Man Innocent

(Washington, DC – July 18, 2002) According to Malcolm Jenkins, attorney of record for Henry Waylon, recently executed for the rape and murder of Colleen Adamson in 1992, DNA evidence obtained by the Innocence Project indicates that his client was in fact wrongfully convicted.

"The tests were concluded only hours after Henry was put to death," Jenkins told this reporter. "They show beyond a shadow of a doubt that not a trace of Henry's DNA was at the scene, and that in fact, it was another unidentified person. The state of Virginia, therefore has killed an innocent man."

While Jenkins's claim cannot be definitely confirmed at this time, a spokesman for the Innocence Project did tell this reporter that the examination of DNA evidence from the crime scene showed that the DNA traces were 'inconsistent with the accused, Henry Waylon.' The spokesman declined to explain further.

In the meantime, the victim's only surviving relative, Yolanda Waylon, had this to say about the case: "Everyone keeps saying that my brother was executed by the state," she said. "But, he was not. He was murdered by the state, and there's no other way to put it." Everyone responsible for this tragedy should be made to pay for it, she also said.

This new finding greatly complicates the state's case, which the State's Attorney's office has always described as 'air tight.' That office has refused to return our calls requesting an interview. The judge who passed sentence

on Waylon ten years ago, State Superior Court Judge
Isaac P. Carson, also declined comment.

"Whew," was all I could say after I'd finished
reading.

"Whew doesn't even begin to cover it,"
Heather said. Her voice quavered. "They just
executed an innocent man."

"That's terrible," I said. "But, mistakes get
made sometimes."

Her eyes blazed pure fury up at me.

"Mistake! You call this a simple mistake?"

I held my hands up in mock surrender.

"Whoa, kid," I said. "I didn't say it was
simple. In fact, there's nothing simple about it
at all. I just said mistakes get made."

"Except, they can't just say, 'oops, sorry,
our bad' can they?"

She had me there. It's one thing to jail an
innocent man. You can release him, apologize
to him; even pay him compensation for the time
he was wrongfully incarcerated. Execute an
innocent person, though, and until we find a
way to pull a Lazarus miracle, you can't
apologize or otherwise make amends.

"No, I guess they can't. Actually, if you must
know, I think it's pretty shitty, but there's
nothing I can do about it, so I'm trying not to
think about it."

She took a deep breath, causing her breasts
to strain against her blouse. For a second I was
afraid the buttons would fly off, but she exhaled
just in time.

"I know you're right," she said. "But, it just
makes my blood boil when something this
wrong happens."

It doesn't exactly make me happy, but like I
said, there's not a lot I can do about it, so I try

to push it out of my mind. I patted her shoulder and went into my office. I threw my jacket at the coat rack. It missed and the damned thing fell into an untidy heap on the floor. I decided not to bother picking it up until I was ready to leave.

It was shaping up to be a truly crappy day.

THREE

My day just sort of went downhill from there.

Quincy's secretary called Heather with a job that needed doing right away.

Quincy Chang is a partner in the law firm, Holcombe, Stein, and Chang, and they have me—now Heather and me—on a ten thousand buck a month retainer. We do mostly the odd investigating job for them, like tracking down heirs to estates to let them know of their good fortune, or finding deadbeat dads, or deadbeat clients. In this case, Quincy wanted me to track down a missing heir who was also a deadbeat.

Just a name, though, was hardly enough to go on, so I called Quincy to get more details. It wasn't all that different from any other trace I'd done, other than the fact that I'd never had to track an heir who also turned out to be a deadbeat.

Edwin Corliss, age 49, was the illegitimate son of a chemical company owner in New Jersey. When the man, whose name wasn't important, died, he finally acknowledged Edwin, and left him five million dollars in his will. The man's legitimate sons had objected, and Edwin had hired Quincy's firm to represent his interests at the probate hearing. When it comes to trial work, there's no one better to represent your interests than Quincy Chang. A third-generation Chinese-American from California, who doesn't speak more than three words of Chinese, Quincy had been a lawyer in the army for fifteen years. He hung up his uniform before I did to pursue a more lucrative career in the civilian world, first as a junior lawyer for Holcombe and Stein, a firm well-known for its hardball tactics on behalf of its clients, and had quickly moved up the ladder, becoming a full partner within three years—a record I've heard. In terms of billable hours; which is how lawyers measure their effectiveness, Quincy had shone as a junior member of the firm, racking up more hours than the next two best. As a full partner, he was even better. At just over six hundred bucks an hour, I estimate that he made the firm nearly a million a year, which explained why they didn't bat an eye when he suggested they retain me at the princely sum of ten grand a month. I've been thinking about asking for a slight raise since Heather is now a full-fledged PI.

At any rate, Edwin Corliss, now five mil richer, owed Holcombe, Stein, and Chang a measly fifteen thousand, and was refusing to pay. His illegitimate half-brothers might not like him, but it was clear that, like them, he'd inherited a miser gene.

The address he'd given Quincy was a post office box in Front Royal, Virginia, but when Quincy's secretary called the Post Office, they'd been unable, or unwilling, to give her an address or phone number, thus I was being sent to the town to track him down and *convince* him that it was best to pay his debts.

I know what you're thinking, and you're wrong. I don't do strong arm work for Quincy. The firm is hard ball, but that's not the way they work. The thinking was that if I could find where he lived, he'd know they could come after him, first with bill collectors, and if that didn't work, a subpoena delivered by a U.S. Marshal, or the local sheriff, informing him that he was being sued by one of the biggest and baddest law firms in Washington, DC. Introducing myself as a representative of that firm would only reinforce the seriousness. At a shade over six feet, and weighing two hundred pounds, with only a slight bit of chunk around the middle, with a chiseled chin, and hard brown eyes, a shade or two darker than my skin—still looking like the Special Forces soldier I'd once been—I'm aware that I can be a bit intimidating when I choose to be.

It was just after nine when I got off the phone with Quincy. Figuring an hour and a half to get to Front Royal, I decided to get that little job out of the way. If things worked out, I could find the guy, pass the message, and get back to DC in time to take Sandra to dinner. The traffic would mostly be DC-bound during my morning drive, and going in the opposite direction on my way back, so barring an accident that tied up traffic in both directions—a common occurrence in the DC area—it would be an easy job.

It hadn't taken me long to get to the I-395 Expressway, but traffic was, as usual, heavy on the westbound inner loop of I-495, so it took me nearly fifteen minutes to get to the exit to I-66 south. It was half past eleven when I took the first exit off I-66 in Front Royal. I hadn't really formulated a plan to find Corliss, and my stomach was growling, so I decided to grab a quick lunch first. There was a barbecue place, *Benny's BBQ*, just off the exit, so I pulled into the parking lot, a bumpy, blacktop, rectangle that surrounded a low-slung corrugated metal building painted red, white, and blue. There were a number of pickups and semis in the parking lot. The place seemed to attract locals as well as truckers. Didn't mean it was any good, but if the food made people sick, the truckers would've spread the word by CB radio and most of them would avoid it.

A hand lettered sign in the window near the entrance said the special of the day was a pulled pork sandwich with coleslaw and a choice of iced tea or lemonade. At $5.95, it sounded reasonable, so I walked to the counter that ran across the back wall, plopped down on one of the fake leather seat stools and rested my elbows on the counter.

A bony woman with a long, narrow nose and stringy brown hair hanging from beneath the hairnet that dug into her broad forehead walked over. She wore a blue dress with a pink apron over it. The red, white, and blue name tag over her small left breast identified her as 'Sally.' She regarded me with watery blue eyes, and picked at a pimple on her chin.

"What can I get you, hon?"

She had a strong southern accent, and made whistling sounds through her nose as she spoke.

"I'll have the special with lemonade," I said.

"Good choice," she said. She turned, and it was then I noticed the narrow slit in the wall behind the counter, with a shelf extending into the dining area as well as into what, from the sizzling and banging sounds, was the kitchen. "Amos, one pulled pork sandwich with coleslaw," she yelled, and then turned back to me. "I'll get your lemonade."

She walked back toward the center of the counter, to a row of taps, took a glass from beneath the counter, filled it halfway with ice cubes, and then filled it with yellowish liquid from the center tap. She brought this back to me, sliding it across the Formica surface until it rested near my elbow.

"Thank you," I said.

"Pleasure, hon," she said.

My sandwich was ready a few minutes later. She took it from the shelf and brought it over to me, placing the large plate next to the lemonade, eying me as she did so. I know I don't look like a trucker, and wasn't a local, so I imagine she was wondering who I was. It gave me an idea. I lifted the lemonade and raised it toward her in a toast.

"Tell me . . . Sally," I said after taking a quick sip. "If I was looking for someone around here, how would I go about finding him?"

"Well, it would depend on why you were looking for him," she said. Her expression was neutral.

I pulled out my wallet and showed her my PI license. "I work for a big law firm in DC, and the person I'm looking for recently came into a large sum of money. He has to sign some papers before the money can be given to him, but the firm didn't have a specific address, just that he lived in Front Royal."

Her eyes narrowed to slits.

"Now, that's right peculiar," she said. "We just recently had a resident who came into some kind of inheritance."

"His name wouldn't be Edwin Corliss, would it," I asked.

"As a matter of fact, it is."

"That's the gentleman I'm looking for."

Now, she was looking suspicious.

"But, I heard he already got his money."

"Well," I said. "He got most of it, but there was a codicil to the will requiring him to sign some kind of statement to get the rest, only in the rush when he was in DC, the firm forgot to get his signature. They wanted to save him another trip north, so they asked me to come and get his signature."

I don't like lying to people, but sometimes it's the kindest thing to do. Besides, most of what I said was true, just that it didn't happen in quite the sequence I was implying.

At any rate, my story seemed to satisfy her. She gave me directions to Corliss' house, actually, she said, it was a double-wide trailer, off Route 340 a few miles north of Front Royal, up some gravel road. Her directions weren't precise, but I thought I'd be able to find the place. I thanked her for the information.

After finishing my sandwich, which was surprisingly good, I called for the check. I gave her a ten and told her to keep the change. She smiled, making her narrow face seem almost pretty.

I drove to Route 340 and turned north. I noticed my tank was just under half full, so I decided to fill up. There just happened to be an Esso station on the right, so I pulled in. The place was run by a swarthy man who looked Indian, but was probably Pakistani. He sat behind a small window with thick glass and a grill set in the center, from where he could see all six pumps. I inserted the hose, locked it, and walked over to the window.

It occurred to me that, next to a waitress in

a local eatery, another person who would know who lived where was a gas station operator. So, I asked the attendant if he knew Edwin Corliss and where he lived. Turned out that almost everyone in town knew Corliss because of his recent inheritance, and that this just happened to be the place where he most often gassed up his pickup. The man gave directions to Corliss' place, which agreed with what Sally the waitress had given me, but with more precise details.

The bell indicating my tank was full rang just as he was finishing his directions. I thanked him, used my credit card to pay for the gas, and took off north again. Following his directions, it only took me fifteen minutes to find the turnoff.

My tires made crackling sounds on the one-lane gravel road that wound through a heavy stand of birch, oak, and maple, interspersed here and there with evergreens. Finally, as it curved right and started up a slight rise, I spotted the double-wide trailer that Corliss called home. It had a dull green roof and yellow walls, both faded from exposure. Large patches of reddish-brown rust dotted the walls. The patches of grass around the trailer hadn't been cut in so long it bent over under the heavy weight of seed pods at the ends. The road petered out fifty feet from the house, turning into gray dirt. A red pickup, more rust-colored from actual rust than red, was parked in front of the awning over the trailer's front door. Off to the right of the trailer was a metal building, about ten feet wide, its walls and roof a shiny silver color. The door of the building was down to within two feet of the ground. I could see the bottom and front tires of a shiny black car, and then I noticed movement—a pair of scuffed brown boots moved across in front of the car.

I drove to the end of the gravel, stopped and turned off the engine. The boots turned to face the door, and stopped moving. I got out of the car.

"Mr. Corliss, Mr. Edwin Corliss," I called.

"Yeah, I'm Ed Corliss," a muffled voice replied. "Who are you and what you want?"

"Mr. Corliss, I'm Al Pennyback," I said. "I work for Holcombe, Stein and Chang, the law firm that represented you. We need to talk."

There was no response. I stood there, my hips against the car door, waiting.

FOUR

After nearly a minute of waiting, the boots took a step forward, and the door began sliding up, making a rumbling sound as it moved along the racks.

Edwin Corliss was displayed piece by piece from the scuffed boots up, and each section was more unappealing than the one before it. His pants, a brown fabric, were ruffled, without a crease of any kind, and hung loosely over his boots. His shirt, which was white once, but was now yellowed with age and who knows what kind of stains, flopped out of his pants and parted in front, pushed out by a gut that was no doubt a result of a taste for beer. He had a round head, with stringy hair that couldn't decide whether it was blond or light brown— what there was of it hung lankly down over his protruding ears, and failed to cover the top of his head. He had light brown eyes, the left one lightly larger than the other and skewed toward the left. As he exited the structure, his mouth opened revealing gaps in his upper jaw. What teeth were left were stained brown and badly in need of the care of a good dentist.

He stood in sharp contrast to the shiny

black Mercedes Benz S500 behind him. All gleaming metal and precision German engineering, it was like seeing a perfectly formed rose in a vase of stinkweed.

He stepped out of the building, turned, and quickly pulled the door down.

"Who'd you say you was again," he asked.

I took my ID out and held it up so he could see it. He leaned forward, squinting at it.

"Okay," he said. "What you want from me?"

"Well, there's the question of the money you owe the law firm."

He scratched at the stubble on his chin.

"Say, would you like a drink," he said.

"No, thank you."

I looked around. There was no way I was drinking anything that came from that place.

"I'm thirsty," he said. "I'm gonna pour myself a little nip."

He went into the trailer. A few minutes later, he came back carrying a bottle of Jack Daniels and two scummy looking water glasses. He put the bottle and glasses down on the dirt, walked around the side of the trailer, and came back a few minutes later with two folding chairs. He handed me one chair, opened the other and plopped down in it. He reached down and picked up the JD and a glass.

"You sure you don't want a taste," he said as he filled his glass almost to the brim.

"No, thanks, I have a long drive back to DC."

"Oh well, all the more for me." He took a long swallow, making smacking and slurping noises. His neck was thick, but I could clearly see his Adam's apple bobbing up and down. He lowered the glass, leaned back against the plastic webbing of the folding chair's back and burped. "Now, that's some good whiskey."

I cleared my throat. "If you don't mind," I said. "I'd like to talk about your debt to Holcombe, Stein, and Chang."

He screwed his eyes up and stared at me over the rim of the glass.

"Now, why in hell I wanta be givin' them hotshot lawyers fifteen thousand dollars," he said, drooling spittle out of the corners of his mouth. "They didn't do all that much."

"Now, I'll be the first to admit that lawyers charge a lot, but you have to admit, their efforts made you five million dollars richer."

"You don't know nothing, fella," he said. "Let me tell you why I don't want to pay these lawyers that much money." And, he began to tell me at length.

Edwin's mother, Zelda Corliss, was an only child of William and Agnes Corliss, poor truck farmers who lived in a double-wide trailer on thirty acres of farmland that didn't make t hem rich, but kept 'body and soul together.' After graduating from high school the year of her nineteenth birthday, Zelda decided enough was enough. She packed a bag, and while her parents were out working the fields, hiked down to the road, hitched a ride into Front Royal, and used the money she'd saved working as a waitress in the barbecue café to buy a ticket on the first bus heading north.

She'd had just enough money to buy a ticket to New Brunswick, New Jersey, but hadn't thought about holding back enough to buy food, so by the end of the two-day trip, her stomach was growling loud enough to annoy her fellow passengers. At the New Brunswick bus terminal, she considered her options, which weren't many. She didn't even have enough money to buy a return ticket to Front Royal.

Having been a good, Christian, God-fearing girl all her life up to that point—meaning that mainly, she'd been to homely for the local boys to care much about, and her parents hadn't let her stray too far from the trailer except to go to school during the week, to her job when she wasn't in school, and to church on Sunday, she'd never considered a life on the shady side of the law. But, desperate times call for desperate measures, and by God, she was starving, and no matter what the preacher said on Sunday, God just wasn't providing. So, she took matters into her own hands, that is, she used her hands to lift the wallet from a prosperous looking passer-by.

She'd never done such a thing before, and was clumsy. Clumsy enough, in fact, that said victim caught her in the act of sliding his stuffed walled from his back pocket. Jonathan Kinswack wasn't a handsome man, but he was rich, and his money had allowed him to marry well, and his wife had dutifully given him two sons. Unfortunately, after the second child, she'd decided enough was enough and closed that department to his operations—so to speak. As a consequence, Jonathan had taken to haunting the area around the bus terminal in search of temporary female companionship. Looking down at Zelda, her wide brown eyes glistening with tears as she shivered, caught dead to rights at her first criminal endeavor, Jonathan was taken by her plight. He was also affected by the sight of her rather large breasts straining against the cheap cotton blouse she wore. So, instead of calling the police and turning her in, he pulled her up and took her to a nearby café, where he bought her supper and listened to her story, which she told between gulping large bites from two hamburgers, two orders of fries, and a super-sized strawberry milkshake.

By the conclusion of her story, and the largest quantity of food he'd ever seen a single woman—especially one her size—consume, Jonathan had made a decision. Since she would need employment in order to live in the city, he offered her a position as a maid and cleaning woman in the large mansion he owned on the outskirts of the city. Having worked for minimum wage at the barbecue joint in her hometown, the two hundred dollars a week he offered her for doing what she'd done at her parents' trailer for free for so many years was like manna from heaven. Jonathan's wife, Muriel, had been happy to have her at first. A rawboned, naïve country girl who followed orders, and was always smiling, relieved her of her household duties, leaving her more time for shopping and playing bridge with her friends. She hadn't even put out too much when she learned that Zelda's duties also included relieving Jonathan's physical 'needs' on occasion. After all, she was only a servant. When Zelda became pregnant, though, Muriel put her foot down. The wretched wench, she said adamantly, would have to go.

Jonathan gave her five hundred dollars and bought her a bus ticket to Front Royal.

Zelda returned home with most of the five hundred and a belly that was already beginning to bulge. Her parents, simple, God-fearing country folks, were devastated, but they loved their simple-minded daughter, so they just kept her in the trailer until Edwin was born. Not that it was a secret. Everyone who mattered had seen Zelda when she stepped off the bus, and they could tell from her belly that she was 'in a family way,' and had no husband.

Not long after his birth, Edwin's grandparents died, leaving Zelda with an infant to fend for herself. She did so, with some difficulty, until Edwin hit eighteen, when she finally gave up and died. That left Edwin, known far and wide as the town 'bastard,' not because of his attitude but because of the circumstances of his birth, with the trailer, the farmland around it, and a well-established aversion to being around other people.

"Mama never did tell me who my pa was," he said when he'd reached the end of his long and rambling story. "Jest that it was some big shot up north. I never knowed nothin' until I got that letter tellin' me I'd come into some money."

He looked down at his glass, now empty, and shook his head. He picked up the bottle of JD and held it up to the light. During the telling of his story he'd gone through at least two glasses, and the light shining through the dark brown square bottle indicated that the level of its contents had dropped to near half. Shaking his head again, he refilled the glass.

"Now that you have the money," I said. "What are your plans?"

He took a long swallow, licked his lips, burped, and looked at me.

"I reckon I done been disrespected by rich folk with their noses in the air lone enough, yessireebob, so now I reckon I can jest tell 'em all to kiss my rosy red ass."

"You think that'll make them respect you?"

"Hell fire, don't everybody respect a man what's got money?"

I didn't want to tell him what many people

thought about most people with money—but, it certainly wasn't respect—I didn't want, though, to turn him away from my main reason for being there.

"So, if it's respect you want," I said. "Why won't you pay what you owe?"

"I just don't like givin' money to them lawyers, is all."

"You know, don't you, that if you refuse to pay, they'll sue you," I said. "That means being served a summons, having to go to court to explain why you haven't paid your bill." His eyes widened, but he'd had so much whiskey he had trouble focusing. "It'll all be public. That won't help your reputation at all."

He'd been standing with his mouth agape. His mouth snapped shut, he blinked, and his mouth drooped open again.

"Uh, guess I hadn't thought about that," he said.

"Yeah, right now, you're probably one of the richest men around here, but if word gets out that you're a deadbeat who doesn't pay his bills, well . . ." I left it hanging there.

His eyes did a little dance in their sockets, a sign, I suppose, that he was thinking and it was a painful operation. Finally, he squinted at me.

"I guess you got a point. Most of these rich bastards are skinflints. Don't reckon I want people to think that of me. How much you say I owe?"

"Fifteen thousand," I said.

"Okay," he said. "You wait here a minute."

The wooden steps made a creaking sound as he entered the trailer. He reemerged a few moments later cradling a shoebox under his arm. When he sat, placed the box on his lap, and opened it, it was my turn to gawk with wide open eyes. It was filled with neatly stacked bundles of money—hundred dollar bills to be exact, and lots of them.

"Uh, do you keep your money in . . . a shoebox under the bed?"

Without looking up at me, he nodded.

"Oh, I jest keep a little spending money here," he said. "Yeah, I keep it under the bed. That's where mama always kept her mad money. Rest is in the bank."

"You're not planning to pay in cash, are you?"

Now he looked at me with his eyes a bit agape.

"Well, sure. What's wrong with that?"

Quincy had said find the guy and try to convince him to pay up. I know he was thinking something along the lines of a bank transfer or a check. But, this was in the middle of the woods in rural Virginia sitting on folding chairs next to a rusty double-wide trailer. And, there was a guy sitting there with a shitload of money in a shoebox. I pulled the pen and notebook from my pocket, the equipment I use to take notes of interviews. Never leave home without them.

"Okay," I said. "I'll write you a receipt, but I need a reliable address so the firm can send you a proper receipt after I turn this in."

"Jest have 'em send it to me general delivery at the Front Royal main post office," he said, as he removed two stacks of bills from the box. He handed me one stack, the band around the bills said it was ten thousand—one hundred 100 dollar bills. He then pulled fifty notes, one at a time, from the second stack, and passed them to me. "Count to make sure I got it right."

I riffed the banded bills and counted the

loose ones—fifteen grand on the nose. I opened the notebook and wrote:

Received from Edwin Corliss of Front Royal, VA
This day July 18, 2002, the sum of
Fifteen thousand dollars---$15,000.00

I signed my name at the bottom, tore the page from the notebook and handed it to him. He glanced at it idly, then folded it and stuffed it into his shirt pocket.

"Thank you, Mr. Corliss," I said. "This should help to keep your reputation up like you want."

He shrugged. "Don't want nobody sayin' Edwin Corliss don't pay his bills."

As I drove away, he was sitting in the folding chair, his feet upon the other, pouring more whiskey into his glass.

FIVE

I stopped at the end of the gravel road and called Quincy. He sounded shocked when I told him I was bringing the money back—in cash—but told me he'd wait in his office to relieve me of it.

The drive back was unpleasant. On the one hand, I wanted to drive fast to get rid of the money, on the other, I feared that I'd get involved in a fender bender and then have to explain all that cash to some Virginia state trooper. Sure, a black guy driving around with fifteen grand in his car, happens every day, no problem. My shirt was soaked with sweat by the time I parked in the basement parking garage of Quincy's building downtown on K Street.

Relieved of the cash, my drive from K Street to the farmhouse, despite the five-thirty rush hour traffic, was like a pleasure cruise.

Sandra was in a much better mood than she'd been in the morning, even going so far as to join me in the shower as I washed the grime from the trip off. Her presence caused my shower to take half an hour longer than usual, but by the time we'd finished, I was squeaky clean, and we'd gotten a head start on the planned after dinner activity.

I'd suggested *Seoul Garden*, off Little River Turnpike in Annandale. We hadn't been there in a while, but we both liked the relatively quiet atmosphere of the place, and the food, if you like Korean food, was great.

The restaurant is a small, one story wooden building on Little River Turnpike, a mile west of I-395. Its dark brown exterior and dark blue tile roof set it apart from the gray concrete and red brick buildings that surround it. It is engulfed on three sides by a large paved parking lot which it shares with an Asian food store and a video shop. It was after seven when we arrived, and the parking lot was only half full, unusual in Korea Town on a Thursday night.

The restaurant itself, when we entered, was also only about half full. The hum of conversation, mostly in Korean, wasn't at the normal decibel level—a quiet Korean restaurant would be considered noisy anywhere else. Believe me, in the normal Korean place, with the loud conversations among the diners and the shouting of the waitresses and cooks you have no choice but to enjoy the food.

A petite young Korean waitress seated us at a table in the front right corner, far from the noise of the kitchen, took our order for two OB beers—a product of the Oriental Brewery, it's one of the first things Korean I experienced when I was assigned there as a young army lieutenant. By the time she was back with two large brown bottles and two glasses, we'd decided on what we wanted to eat, so she took our order. Sandra had convinced me that we should eat light, since we'd be having barbecue with Buster and his family that coming weekend, so I ordered *kalbi*, which is boneless beef rib meat, sliced about 1/8 inch thick and is cooked on a gas-fired grill that sits in the center of the table. Along with the *kalbi*, we had the fiery fish soup, *mae-un tang*, white rice, and about ten different kinds of *kim-chi*, the traditional Korean side dish, which ranges from the foul-smelling winter *kim-chi*—which we passed on—to spicy fermented radish and garlic, to mild *mulkim*-chi, radish slices in water.

Because this was a cook-at-the-table meal, it came quickly. The waitress, who didn't seem to understand or speak much English, began cutting up the beef with a large pair of what looked like dressmaker's shears, and putting the pieces on the hot grill, which she'd greased with a piece of fat. She added a few cloves of garlic to the grill, stirring them around so the flavor would get into the meat. While she cooked, Sandra and I attacked the fish soup, pausing frequently to spoon rice into our mouths to ease the burn from the fiery red pepper powder suspended in the liquid.

The waitress began flipping dark brown pieces of beef onto the plates in front of us just about the time we'd decided in the battle between our tongues and the soup, the soup had won hands down.

We began the rather elaborate process of eating the *kalbi*, which involved smearing a brown bean paste on a lettuce leaf, adding a dollop of rice, a piece of *kalbi*, a clove of garlic, a piece of sliced green pepper and a bit of *kim-chi*, rolling it all into a ball and stuffing it into your mouth. It sounds messy, but it's delicious and actually fun once you get the hang of it.

As I was stuffing the second lettuce ball into my mouth, my gaze was caught by one of the TV sets mounted high on the walls around the place. It was tuned to one of the local Washington area news stations. I couldn't hear the announcer, an attractive blonde with shiny hair that looked glued in place, but the crawl at the bottom of the screen caught my eye:

DNA Results Indicate Waylon Was Innocent!

Sandra must have caught the look of surprise on my face. She turned just before the crawl moved on to something else. When she turned back she had a stricken expression on her face.

"Who was it that said Justice is blind," she asked. "She must be to allow an innocent man to be put to death."

The next sentence moved onto the screen.

No comments from Va. Governor's Office.

No surprise there. The suits surrounding his honor the governor were probably huddling trying to come up with a damage control plan. Opponents of the death penalty had often used the specter of the government executing an innocent person, while death penalty supporters claimed that such fears were overblown. This one would have everyone's tits in a ringer for sure.

For Sandra, though, it was personal. We'd met when a kid she taught was gunned down in the streets, and the police, mainly because the kid was black, had written it off as just another street gang incident. That it had later turned out the boy had been murdered by a gang of art thieves—all white—because he'd accidentally seen them moving some of their stolen merchandise, hadn't made as many headlines as the gang theory had.

I wondered how long the Waylon case would hold anyone's attention.

SIX

After stuffing our faces with Korean food, Sandra and I got home just before eleven and by mutual consent, showered and hit the sack.

I woke up at 5:00 am to the sound of the air conditioning, already straining to cope with the rising temperature, a sign that the day would be a scorcher.

That feeling was further reinforced when I rolled out of bed and my bare feet hit the floor. Normally, the bedroom's wooden floor is cool to the touch at that time of morning, but this morning, it felt like lukewarm water. Sighing, I got up and padded to the bathroom to relieve myself.

Afterwards, I stripped and pulled on my lightweight gray sweats. While I was sitting on the edge of the bed lacing up my running shoes, Sandra woke up and turned over.

"Don't leave without me," she said. She sat up, stretched and got out on her side. I stopped lacing my shoes long enough to watch the undulating movement of her hips through the white t-shirt that clung to them, only resuming my lacing when she closed the bathroom door.

I sat there on the edge of the bed until I heard the toilet flush. A few minutes later she came out. She pulled the t-shirt off, revealing her beautiful, athletic body—but, only for a moment. She quickly donned a sweat suit similar to mine except that where mine looked baggy hers clung to every delicious curve. After putting on her new pink top running shoes, she stood and stretched. We then went out and did our four-mile run through the woods, worked out twenty minutes on the heavy bag in the barn where I was still teaching her taekwondo—she'd moved way beyond the basic moves, and was now able to give me a run for money when we sparred, and then I meditated while she showered.

After she finished showered, I took my turn under the hot water. It was her turn to do breakfast.

I dressed in dark green cotton pants and a matching short sleeve shirt. An olive drab cotton jacket with sleeve pockets completed the ensemble. Sandra gave me a raised eyebrow and air kiss as I entered the kitchen. She was at the stove, deftly flipping pancakes onto a platter. I walked up behind her and kissed her lightly on the back of her neck.

"No distractions, big fella," she said. "I have to pay careful attention to these pancakes." Her words were negated by the way she thrust her hips back against me.

I pulled back. "Can't have that," I said. "Need any help?"

She looked over her shoulder at me. "How about setting the table . . . oh, and could you turn the radio on, I'd like to catch the news?"

The radio was on the counter near the sink, but hard to reach from the stovetop island. I walked past her and turned it on. The announcer, a woman with a plummy English accent, was well into the morning broadcast, ". . . has been opposed to the court since its establishment July first. The Congress is considering legislation to prevent the U.S. from becoming a member.

"South African President Thabo Mbeki, the first president of the recently established African Union, is in Addis Ababa, Ethiopia today to participate in ceremonies surrounding the opening of the new body's headquarters there.

"In local news, while local human rights groups and anti-death penalty activists are up in arms over the recent execution of Henry Waylon, a young black college student who was convicted of the rape and murder of 16-year-old Colleen Adamson in 1992, but who has since been deemed innocent based on recently analyzed DNA evidence, the state of Virginia has remained silent on the case. In a related bit of news, Gunther Weiss, age 72, who was the foreman of the jury that convicted Waylon, was found dead in his home in Alexandria's Mount Vernon area early this morning. Mr. Weiss, who, according to his family physician, had a history of heart ailments, is believed to have died of a heart attack.

"That's it for National Public Radio News for this morning. Stay tuned for Car Talk coming up. We'll have more news at noon on this, your local NPR station."

A male voice, this time with a nasal Midwestern accent, began reciting a list of the people and organizations who had so kindly donated to make the broadcasts possible, and encouraging listeners to be equally generous. We tuned it out as we ate breakfast, pancakes, eggs over easy, and ham. Sandra had decided to brew Jamaican coffee instead of Colombian. It went well with the pancakes.

After breakfast, since it was early, and I didn't think there'd be much to do at the office, we made a detour through the bedroom for a little morning cuddling, which lasted thirty minutes. As a result, it was half past nine when I arrived.

Heather gave me an aggrieved look when I walked in.

"I'm not even going to ask why you're late," she said. "That 'cat who ate the canary' grin on your face says it all. You had a call . . . several calls in fact . . . from a judge, Isaac Carson, and he wants you to call him back. He said it was urgent."

The name didn't register at first, but as I took the square sticky pad note with the number it hit me.

"Say, that's the judge in that case of the kid who was recently executed, isn't it?"

"One and the same."

"I wonder why he'd want to talk to me."

"There's only one way to find out." She cocked her head, giving me a 'poor baby' look that from someone else would have been really annoying.

"Okay, I'll call him."

In my office, I hung my jacket on the rack, sat down behind my desk, causing the leather on my second-hand leather executive chair to squeak, and looked around.

I was putting off making the call. I wasn't sure why I didn't want to do it. Ordinarily, I pay little attention to my office. It is, after all, just an office, a place where I hang out a few hours a day, five days a week, waiting for someone to need my services. It's pretty bare bones. My desk, an old government issue wooden thing that I picked up at a government surplus auction along with the chair, a couple of low book cases containing phone books and a few reference manuals that I hardly ever read, and a single, straight back chair at the left side of my desk for visitors. The walls were the same faint green color as those in the outer office where Heather sat, but where her walls were covered with calendars, brightly colored pictures of flowers, cats, and other creatures, I had a couple of hunting prints—that Heather had found somewhere and insisted that I let her hang—and a color photo of me with former Chairman of the Joint Chiefs of Staff General Colin Powell, taken when I was serving in the Pentagon just before retirement. I no longer remembered what the occasion for the photo had been, but the general had kindly signed it, 'to Al with best wishes, Colin Powell.' It was one of the few things from my time in the army I ever displayed. Too many memories that I wanted not to remember tied up with most of the others.

The view out the one window had in better times been of the Washington Channel and the Potomac River beyond. But, that had long since been replaced with a view of the glass, steel and concrete sides of the condos that loomed over us, so I usually didn't even bother looking for the sliver of a view that could be glimpsed between the buildings when autumn and winter stripped the trees of their leaves.

That left, of course, nothing else to do but call Carson and find out why he wanted to talk to me. What would a judge in Virginia need from a private investigator in the District of Columbia?

Well, as Heather said, only one way to find out. I put the sticky note on my desk, smoothing it out, and dialed the number.

"Yes, may I help you?" The voice, smooth and deep, like a jazz or blues singer, answered after two rings.

"Is this Judge Carson?" I asked.

"Yes, it is. Who is this?"

"Al Pennyback, judge. You left a message with my partner that you wanted to speak with me."

"Mr. Pennyback. Good of you to return my call. I was wondering if I might speak personally with you."

I'm a sucker for puzzles, and my curiosity antenna was buzzing.

"This isn't something we could discuss over the phone?"

There was a moment of silence. When he finally spoke, I could hear the tension in his voice.

"No," he said slowly. "It's something I can only discuss in private. When could you come to see me?"

Clients weren't exactly lining up outside my office. In other words, I could go and see him at any time.

"I guess I could drop by your office this morning. What's a good time for you?"

"Could you make it by eleven? And, I'd rather you came to my home rather than my office." He gave me an address in Alexandria, in the area not far from Mount Vernon.

"Okay, I'll be there at eleven." I was vaguely familiar with the area. Lots of big, expensive houses, most with locked gates and not very welcoming security company signs. "Will I have any problem getting in?"

"There's a speaker at the gate. Just press the buzzer and announce yourself when you arrive. I'll let you in."

Without waiting for me to acknowledge his instructions, he hung up.

I sat there for a few minutes staring at the phone. The judge was scared of something. But, why in hell was he calling me about it?

SEVEN

I left the office at 10:15, and it took me the whole time until 11:00 to get to the address in Alexandria, just off the George Washington Memorial Parkway, about a quarter mile west of Fort Hunt National Park, and about an equal distance east of Mount Vernon, home of our first president.

The house wasn't visible from the street because of the ten foot high brick wall that surrounded it. The gate, an iron monstrosity with golden filigree and spikes in the top was set back in an alcove about ten feet deep near the front center of the wall. My Volkswagen felt positively tiny sitting there with the walls looming over us on both sides and the big black gate to the front.

I rolled the window down and leaned out to press a button on the black box atop a black metal post on the left. It made a beeping sound followed by, "Yes?" the judge's voice, though a bit tinny from the tiny speaker was nonetheless recognizable. I identified myself. He didn't say anything, but the speaker made a popping sound, and there was a loud buzz, and the gate swung inward like the batwing doors of an old west saloon.

I drove quickly up a winding driveway that was flanked on both sides by hardwood trees like gray-clad sentinels clasping green-sleeved hands overhead. In a few places the sun broke through spaces in the leaves, painting light patterns on the macadam surface.

The driveway curved around and under a porte cochere whose white columns supported a roofed balcony. The house was pastel blue, with white trim and dark blue roof slates. Round turrets with steeply pitched conical roofs stood at each corner. The house was surrounded by neatly trimmed hedges and flowers. The driveway went on past the porte cochere, looping around upon to meet itself. A large rectangular concrete pad in front of a three-car garage off the left hand side of the loop I took to be where guests parked.

As I pulled into the area farthest from the garage and got out, I noticed that the trees blocked the view of the street and sides of the property. I imagined it was the same in back, leaving me wondering why rich people spent so much money building fancy looking houses and then hid them from view.

Shaking my head, I walked to the front door. Off-white marble steps, two of them, led up to the arched double doors, blonde wood with cut glass panes. I thumbed the doorbell. Chimes inside the house sounded the opening notes of *fur Elise.*

Through the thick panes of glass I could

see a wavery figure approaching, all black and white. The left hand door swung inward. A dark brown woman, about five-three and stickily built, dressed in a black and white maid's uniform like someone out of a B-movie, looked up at me with a stern look.

"Can I help you?" she asked in a deep voice. She had a slight southern accent, and humorless brown eyes.

"I have an appointment with Judge Carson."

She squinted at me, her frown deepening. Just then, a tall man with even darker skin, a square jaw, thick white mustache, and close-cropped white hair, wearing a dark blue jacket that stretched across his ample middle, stepped through a door to the right and up behind the woman.

"That's alright, Mabel," he said in a deep, sonorous voice. "I'm expecting Mr. Pennyback."

I looked at him with raised brows.

"I've seen your photo in the *Post*, Mr. Pennyback," he said, his full lips curving slightly upward. "Unlike most people, you're larger than your pictures would indicate. Please, come in."

The woman made a sniffing noise and stepped aside. Carson turned and headed back toward the door that he'd come through without waiting to see if I would follow. I shrugged and followed. The room he'd entered was larger than my office. It had a large polished wood desk off to one side, with a high-back leather upholstered chair behind it. A gooseneck lamp cast a circle of light on the shiny surface of the desk. Behind the desk was a floor to ceiling book case that covered the entire wall. It was filled with impressive looking books, many with what looked like leather binding. To the right was a low, kidney-shaped coffee table, with high-back chairs at the narrow ends and a high-back love seat against the wall facing the long side. On the table was a silver tray and coffee urn surrounded by two expensive looking cups and saucers and a matching cream and sugar set. The small silver spoons looked just as expensive. The lighting in the room was soft, but sufficiently bright that everything, including two small paintings that looked like the real deal, could be clearly seen.

Carson sat on the farthest chair and motioned me to the love seat. I sat facing him in the other chair. He frowned.

"Would you care for coffee?" he asked.

I nodded. When he pushed the sugar and cream containers my way, I shook my head. "I take mine black." I took a sip of the coffee. It was delicious. "This is good. Colombian isn't it?"

He smiled. "You know your coffee. I have five pounds flown up every month from Bogota."

"That must be pretty expensive. I get mine at a local store in one pound bags, and they cost nearly twelve bucks each."

"Yes, I suppose." He shrugged. "But, what price tag can one put on such a thing?"

Whatever that meant. I guess judges made more than I thought. This house, specially imported coffee, and his suit looked like it cost more than I made in a month.

"Sure," I said. I took another sip. It *was* good. "Now, if we could get to business. Why did you want to see me?"

"Ah, yes, that. I've been led to understand that you're the best at what you do."

"Well, if you mean tracking down missing heirs or deadbeats who don't want to pay their bills, I guess I am pretty good."

He put his cup down and stared at me intently. He leaned forward with his large hands resting on the knees of his expensive coal gray slacks.

"You're far too modest, Mr. Pennyback," he said. "I happen to know that you've solved a number of cases that had the police puzzled. You're known as something of a white knight when it comes to aiding those in need. I also know that you're considered pretty tenacious when you're following leads . . . need I go on?"

Okay, he had me there. I do tend to be a pit bull when a puzzle has attracted my attention. I held up a hand in surrender.

"Okay, I guess you're right on all counts, but it's not white knight . . . the *Post* calls me the Brown Knight." I chuckled. "Lucy Garcia, the reporter who came up with that nickname, is sort of a friend of mine."

"Ah, yes . . . the Brown Knight . . . an interesting sobriquet. Perhaps a bit politically incorrect in today's age, but I can see how it might resonate with certain people."

No kidding, that's how the guy talked. It was like listening to someone read the dictionary, and with that 'James Earl Jones as Darth Vader' voice of his . . . well, it was a bit creepy really.

"I try to ignore it," I said. "But, look, you didn't ask me here to discuss my press coverage. Why did you want to talk to me?"

He looked at me, his dark brown eyes

boring through me with a focus like a laser. I would have thought he was trying to be intimidating if not for the way his large fingers massaged his knees, putting slight wrinkles in his pants.

Finally, his fingers stopped moving. His expression softened into a kind of sad look.

"I find, Mr. Pennyback, that I am in need of your services."

"We, that is, my partner and I, don't do domestic cases."

He looked confused, and then a hint of anger creased his features.

"You misunderstand me . . . I have no need of a service like . . . I mean . . . I need your skills as an investigator to *identify* someone."

"Oh." That was all I could think of to say at first. I don't usually jump to conclusions, and in the rare cases that I do, the pool is usually empty and I land square on my face. I took a second to gather myself. "I'm sorry, you're right, I guess I did misunderstand," I said. "It's just that I've never had a judge need my services before. After all, you have the police department and the office of the district attorney available to you. What could I provide that they can't?"

"Discretion, Mr. Pennyback, discretion," he said. He looked sad. "I guess I can see how you might have come to the conclusion you did. But, I assure you, I have no need for *that* kind of investigation. I'm a widower . . . my wife of thirty years passed away five years ago after a long bout with breast cancer. I've never remarried, and really have no social life to speak of."

"My apologies for making a stupid

assumption, your honor, and my condolences—as belated and useless as they are. But, I don't understand . . . what do you mean by discretion?"

He looked around as if to make sure no one was listening. I began to get an itchy feeling at the back of my neck. When people do that I'm seldom pleased by what they have to say next.

Finally, he leaned forward, and spoke in a low voice. "As you might imagine," he said. "There are not all that many African-American judges in Commonwealth of Virginia courts, hardly any at all with my seniority."

He took a sip of coffee.

"Right now, I'm being considered for a seat on the U.S. District Court. There are many of my fellow jurists who would like to see that seat go to someone else. Any hint of scandal or weakness on my part could doom my candidacy."

"I still don't see what that has to do with me," I said. "I don't cover up scandals."

"I do not want you to cover up a scandal." He sat back in his chair. "In fact, I can tell you, in all my years on the bench, there's never been even a hint of impropriety."

All I could do was sit there looking confused. Not a pleasant situation, I can tell you, but I couldn't even begin to guess what he was talking about.

He shrugged, giving me a look like I was a dimwitted school boy who wasn't understanding a simple math problem.

"Very well," he continued. "Let me see if I can make it very clear. I need you to find out who is threatening me."

Oh, is that all? It still didn't make a lot of sense.

"Someone's threatening you? Who, and about what? Why not just take it to the police? If not the locals, certainly the state police would be interested. Hell, even the FBI might be concerned about someone making threats against a sitting judge."

"I wish it was that simple," he said. He sighed heavily. "If this gets out, however, it would give my opponents more than enough ammunition to destroy me. If I go to the authorities, there's no way it can be kept quiet, you see."

I was beginning to get it—or thought I was.

"You want me to identify this person threatening you . . . and then, what?"

His mouth opened in a surprised circle. "Uh, well, I hadn't really thought about that. I . . . what . . . if you should find this person, what would you recommend I do?"

Boy, rich people can be so clueless. So accustomed to just giving orders or wishing for something; give them a real problem and they're totally helpless. They're so separated from the real world that the rest of us inhabit.

"I hate to be the one to tell you this, but if the threats are real, you'll have to take it to the authorities."

He blinked and stared at me, his mouth agape.

"B-but . . . that would mean . . ."

"Yes," I said. "That would mean the whole thing would likely come out. But, if the threat is real, the alternative could be worse. Speaking of that, what makes you think you're being threatened in the first place?"

He reached into his jacket, and after hesitating a moment, pulled out a single sheet of paper. He handed it across to me.

"This was delivered to my office at the courthouse this morning, just before I called you. Someone put it in the pile of interoffice mail."

I took the paper and laid it on the table, smoothing it out. It looked like common printer paper, the kind you buy by the box at Office Depot, and the letters on it were a common font used by the small desktop printers you see all over the place. The message, though, was pretty graphic,

> YOU SENT AN INNOCENT MAN
> TO HIS DEATH, AND FOR THAT
> YOU SHOULD FORFEIT YOUR
> OWN LIFE. SLEEP WITH YOUR
> EYES OPEN FROM NOW ON.

The note wasn't signed or dated. It was hard to know whether it was serious or just someone playing a prank.

"You've handled this," I said. "Did anyone else in your office touch it?"

"My secretary and the receptionist at the front desk handled the envelope. As far as I know I'm the only one who handled the letter itself.

"Well, the first thing that needs to be done is to have it dusted for fingerprints. I could check for fingerprints, but I don't have any way of checking the fingerprint data bases to try and identify who the prints belong to."

His face fell. "So, you're telling me that the only thing I can do is go to the police, or sit and wait for whoever sent this to make good on the threat?"

"It would look like that. It wouldn't hurt if you could give them some idea of who the author of this might be."

"Honestly, I haven't a clue," he said.

Whenever anyone starts a sentence with the word 'honestly,' there's a good chance they're about to tell you a lie. When they quickly avert their gaze and refuse to look you in the eye, as Carson did, the chance of their statement being a lie goes up exponentially. I don't like rich people very much, and this case didn't look like one that I could do much with. Him lying to me was just the final straw.

"Well, your honor," I said. "I'm afraid there's nothing I can do for you. I don't have the resources to properly analyze that note, and since you're so set against involving the authorities, I don't see how I could take your case. I'm sorry."

"I wish you would think about it before making a final decision." There was a pleading note in his voice. "At least give it 24 hours. Please, I need your help, Mr. Pennyback."

All I wanted to do at that moment was get the hell out of there. But, I'd always been taught to be polite—even to rich people.

"Okay, judge. I'll think on it and call you tomorrow."

"That's all I can ask of you," he said.

He rose and extended a hand. I grasped it. His grip was firm and dry.

I left him standing there, a forlorn look on his face.

EIGHT

Back at the office I told Heather what had happened, and my decision not to take the case. She frowned at me.

"I think you're wrong," she said.

"Wrong . . . about what?"

I grasped the back of the chair I'd been straddling and scooted it back away from her desk a few inches. Heather never hesitated to disagree with me when she thought I was wrong, but I'd never heard her do it in quite so strong a voice.

She tapped the eraser of her pencil against her chin. The intense look in her blue eyes had me feeling I was about to be impaled.

"Well, for starters," she finally said. "You have a reputation of being there for people in need, and it sounds like the judge is a person in need." She raised one finger. "Secondly, this is a mystery . . . an anonymous threat, an unidentified perpetrator . . ." A second finger was raised. "What more do you need? This sounds to me like a case that's right up your alley."

I raised my right hand, traffic cop style.

"Yeah, but this guy's the judge that sent an innocent man to his death. How do you think it would go down in the local community if it was learned I'd been helping him?"

She tapped the pencil again. "Well, some of them might be a tad upset." Tap, tap. "But, they know your reputation, and in the end would realize that you did the right thing."

I was determined not to be railroaded on this. A nagging feeling in my lizard brain was trying to tell me to stay far away from Judge Carson and his problems—or, that's how I was interpreting my uneasy feeling.

"But, the guy didn't give me anything useful to go on," I said. "An unsigned note that's probably got who knows who's fingerprints on it, which I don't have the capacity to identify anyway, and-"

"You've never let things like that stop you in the past," she said. She'd stopped tapping the pencil against her chin and was pointing it at me. "How would you feel if this threat turns out to be real, and something happened to the judge?"

"Probably half as bad as I felt when I heard the news that a young man was executed and, oops, turns out he was innocent. Don't forget who sentenced that young man to die."

I hadn't realized it until I said it, but Henry Waylon's death had bothered me more than even I thought at first. And *that* was the thing that was making me feel uneasy. Why in hell would I want to help the guy who had sentenced an innocent young man to be strapped to a gurney and have his veins filled, first with pentobarbital to render him unconscious, then pancuronium bromide to paralyze the breathing muscles, and finally potassium chloride to stop his heart. I've never witnessed an execution, and while this procedure is supposed to be 'humane,' I can imagine that if not enough of the first drug's administered, the second and third must cause pain and induce panic in those final moments before a prisoner dies. His involvement in Waylon's death, along with the fact that he was a part of that privileged elite, that percent of the population that has so much control over the rest of us, while not giving a damn really about us—well, let's just say the good judge wasn't my cup of tea.

None of that had any impact on Heather. The woman is a dyed in the wool bleeding heart liberal. Her heart's bigger than Alaska. It really doesn't matter; stray dog or rich judge in need, it's Heather Bunche to the rescue. Well, actually, it's Al Pennyback to the rescue, but it's Heather who shoves me out the door.

"Okay," she said. "I'll grant you, that bothers me a little, but it doesn't change the fact that someone's threatening the poor man, and he can't really go to the authorities about it."

I raised a finger; then pointed it at her.

"Someone is *allegedly* threatening him. For all we know, this could be a ruse to arouse sympathy to get him that job on the federal court."

She put a finger to her lips.

"Oh, I hadn't thought about that." Then

her expression brightened. "No, that makes no sense. You'd pretty quickly discover that, and knowing you it wouldn't go well for the judge after you did. He sounds like a pretty smart man to me, so it's for sure he's done his homework and knows what kind of man you are. I don't think it's a ruse. I think that he *thinks* someone's threatening him."

"I'm still not sure," I said. "Besides, how are we supposed to determine the sender of that note? We don't have access to fingerprint data bases."

"Maybe we don't, but I have friends who do."

Heather, in addition to her computer skills, has an address file that includes the secretaries, personal assistants, and confidential aides of nearly everyone in Washington who matters, other than the president—and, sometimes I'm not sure she doesn't have the number of someone in the White House. If there's anyone who can get access to government resources, the name's probably in Heather's file.

"Okay, okay, let's say I decide to take the job. What the hell do you suggest I do?"

"Hey, you're the experienced detective in this partnership," she said. "If you didn't have this blind spot about the guy being rich . . . let's just say he was an ordinary citizen . . . what would you do?"

That was easier said than done. I'd been to his house, and he *was* rich, or at least he certainly had all the trappings of a very rich person. I took a deep breath. What *would* I do if he'd been a grocery store clerk, and he was being threatened by some nut that sent anonymous notes?

"Well, I guess the first thing I'd do is talk to him. See if he had any ideas as to who might want to do him harm.

Her head bobbed up and down, causing her hair, as short as it was, to sway from side to side.

"Then, I'd get that note and see if we could trace the sender."

I didn't hold out much hope there. She didn't either apparently. She frowned, but kept bobbing her head affirmatively.

"I guess that would be two good places to start," she said. "What next?"

Damned if I wasn't beginning to feel like she was tutoring me, rather than the other way around. I could also see that she was using a technique I'd used myself on occasion. She was letting me talk myself into taking the damn case. And, it was working. I was already halfway there.

` "Okay, I'd start talking to the people whose names he gave me." She raised an eyebrow. "Oh yeah, and I'd get a list of people close to him, whether he thought they were potential threats or not, and I'd talk to them."

"That's what you've always taught me. So, what's your next step?"

I made a growling sound deep in my throat. I stood up and went into my office. As I picked up the phone, I thought about how I'd just been so skillfully maneuvered. Heather was becoming a first rate private eye. I dialed the number. It rang twice.

"Yes," the deep voice said.

"Judge Carson," I said. "Al Pennyback here. I'll take your case. Will you be home around 1:30?"

NINE

I drove to Fort McNair and had lunch at the officer's club, a two story red brick building near the center of the post that dated from the 1860s. After lunch, drove back to Carson's mansion.

It took some pressing, but I finally got him to admit that he thought Henry Waylon's sister, Yolanda, was most likely the author of the note. She was fifteen at the time of his conviction, and had made a scene in the court room during sentencing, and had to be forcibly removed by the bailiff. The other possibility, he thought, would be the condemned man's girlfriend, Penelope Payton, who had insisted throughout that he was innocent, but who hadn't been able to give him a solid alibi for the time of the crime. Beyond that, he knew of a few other relatives or close friends of people he'd passed judgement on, but couldn't be absolutely sure. He also gave me the note.

I informed him that my partner would do a contract for his signature and get it to him by the next day for signature. When I told him our fees, five hundred a day plus expenses, he didn't even blink. I asked for a two thousand dollar retainer, and he took a checkbook from the desk in his study and, using an expensive gold Parker pen, wrote a check.

I still wasn't happy about the case, but the money wouldn't hurt our bank account.

Back at the office, I gave the note and list of names to Heather.

"It would be nice," I said. "Just in case you can't find fingerprints, if you could ID the paper and printer."

She held it up to the light and peered at it.

"That's not going to be easy. I can tell this is common printer paper, the kind you get for nine bucks a box of 3,000 sheets at Office Depot and the printing looks like anyone of a hundred of small office printers."

"Well, give it a try anyway."

"Of course I will."

"Run each of these names, but pay close attention to the top two, Yolanda Waylon and Penelope Payton," I said. "In fact, if you could get a quick address on Ms. Waylon, I'd like to talk to her as soon as possible."

"I'm on it," she said, and turned her attention to her computer screen.

When Heather says she's on something, she's quite literal. She had Yolanda Waylon's work and home address within twenty minutes. I'm still reluctant to ask her how she does it. I just hope it's legal.

She lived in a small condo near 4th and I Streets, just east of Southeastern University, in area that was being rapidly gentrified. She worked as a lab technician at a place called MedGen, located on Bashford Lane near the railroad tracks in Alexandria.

MedGen was in a two-story rectangular building made of some kind of off-white stone. The ground floor had no windows, just a double glass door in the center. The second floor had large windows at the right side, but was windowless on the left. A large parking lot that enclosed the building separated it from neighboring structures. A large sign at the entrance to the parking lot directed visitors to a small number of slots about thirty feet from the front entrance. I wasn't sure if this was for convenience of visitors, or to enable the people inside to more effectively monitor visitors. My gut told me it was the latter.

There was a clicking sound as I approached the glass door. I put a hand on the bar across the middle and pushed. It swung silently inward.

The reception area was large, with a high desk to the right, behind which sat a statuesque black woman with close cropped, shiny black hair and a no nonsense expression on her mocha colored face. Her uniform, which accented the curves of her generous breasts, was dark blue with red piping. To the left were several groupings of plastic chairs and tables. Magazines and newspapers were scattered casually on the tables. I hadn't seen the cameras, but as I approached the desk, I could see the top of a bank of monitors. From where she sat, the receptionist had a view of most of the complex.

"May I help you?" Her light brown eyes gave me a thorough inspection.

I showed her my ID and asked if I could

speak with Yolanda Waylon. She asked me why, and I gave her the spiel about client confidentiality and all that. She made a sound like 'hmph,' and told me to have a seat.

The reception area took up, I estimated, about the middle third of the front section of the building. I hadn't been able to get a good look at the side, but the from thirty foot distance from the front door to the back wall, I estimated that there'd be a fairly sizable room behind it as well. The back wall was a mural—a view of Washington, DC from the Virginia side of the Potomac, with the Lincoln Memorial and Washington Monument near the center, and the Capitol Dome in the background. From the pink blossoms on the trees around the buildings to the right, it looked like spring, which is one of the prettiest times to be in the nation's capital, unless you suffer from pollen allergies.

What I didn't see in the any of the walls was a door to the rest of the building. So, I was a bit surprised when a rectangle just off the left center of the mural opened and a woman walked through into the reception area. She wore pink hospital scrubs that didn't hide the fact that she had small breasts and slightly wide hips. Her dark brown hair was cut short and clung to her oval head. I got a quick glance at her face before she turned toward the receptionist. She had a thin nose, full lips, and oval shaped eyes. She walked with a confident stride. If she'd been a man I would have said she was former military.

"Who wants to see me, Rachael?" she asked in a husky voice.

The receptionist pointed toward me.

"Dude over there, Yolanda, says he's a private investigator named Albert E. Pennyback . . . at least that's what on his ID."

Yolanda Waylon turned and squinted at me, her lips turned down in a half frown. Slowly, she walked toward me. I stood.

About four feet away from me she stopped. I extended my hand to shake, but she didn't close the distance to take it.

"Who are you, and why do you want to talk to me?"

"Yolanda Waylon," I said. "The sister of Henry Waylon?"

At his name, she winced. Her lips trembled and her eyes glistened, but she didn't cry. She took a deep breath.

"Yeah, Henry is . . . was my brother. Why the fuck would a private investigator want to talk to me about him?"

"Is there some place we can talk privately?" I asked.

"Why? Everyone here knows about Henry. He's dead already, so why would you need privacy to talk about him?"

There was a slight tremor in her voice, but from the determined set of her jaw, I think it was more from anger than anything else.

"Trust me, Ms. Waylon . . . the matter I need to discuss is private. I'm truly sorry for your loss. What was done to your brother was really a tragedy. But, what I'm trying to do is prevent another tragedy. If I could just have a few minutes of your time."

She cocked her head to one side and looked at me. It felt like she was looking right into my mind. I don't know what she saw, but she finally shrugged her shoulders causing her tiny breasts to jiggle under her top.

"We can talk over in the far corner," she said. "The acoustics are pretty lousy in here, so unless someone's sitting right next to us or we shout, no one will here." She turned to the receptionist. "Rachael, Mr. Pennyback and I need some privacy. Could you make sure no one bothers us?"

"You got it, honey."

She led me to a table with two chairs in the back left corner of the room. She motioned toward the chair facing the wall, and went around the table and sat in the other. I moved the empty chair around until the side wall was behind me, and she was near at my left.

"You were in the army, weren't you?" she asked.

"Yes, yes I was. How'd you know?"

"That thing with the chair. When I was in the army, a lot of the guys I knew who'd been in the Rangers did that. Never liked to have their backs to a door."

So, she *had* been in the military. I mentally kicked myself for the implied sexism in my not having immediately realizing that.

"Yeah, I guess it is a silly habit," I said. "But, it saved my life on a couple of occasions."

She smiled for the first time, creating little dimples in both cheeks. She wasn't unattractive, but when she smiled, her whole face lit up, making her downright pretty.

"Nothing silly about it," she said. "It's always better to be able to see your surroundings. Now, what is it you want to talk to me about?"

"I'd like to talk to you about your brother's . . . case-"

"My brother's case?" Her eyes blazed with sudden anger, and red circles appeared on her cheeks. "You mean my brother's murder! That's right; he was *murdered* by the state of Virginia. What else do you call it when an innocent man is killed?"

I couldn't really disagree with her, but that wasn't the reason I was there. I needed to get a sense if she was the one threatening the good judge, and if she was, just how far she might be willing to go to carry out a threat. I was already getting a sense that she had enough anger, but anger alone wasn't enough. I decided to try and calm her down.

"Right, your brother's murder," I said. "You're absolutely right. That's why I'm against capital punishment. It's not like you can mistake, realize it, and open a cell door and say, 'sorry, we goofed, you're free to go. You have every right to be mad as hell about it."

"Fucking-A right I do. Henry and I've been saying for the last ten years that he didn't rape and kill that girl, but did they listen? No. Hell, they had him fitted for the gurney from the moment they arrested him. Nice little white girl gets herself killed, and there's this uppity ni-, black boy with no alibi. It was a slam dunk."

"What evidence did they have against your brother?"

She closed her eyes and wrinkled her brow. The pained look when she opened her eyes said that this wasn't a pleasant conversation.

"It was all circumstantial," she said. "He was over in Rosslyn with some of his classmates from George Washington University. He was a pre-med student there. He'd been seen talking to this girl, who was underage and shouldn't even have been there, in the bar where they were drinking. When she was found raped and strangled under the Virginia side of Key Bridge, the cop in charge of the investigation keyed in on Henry. Hell, that bastard didn't even seriously consider that it could have been anyone else . . . Henry was the only black face in that bar that night, so-"

"A case of pretty serious racial profiling," I said. "I hate to say it, but it happens. But, surely they had some other evidence."

"Well, according to witnesses, Henry and the girl left the bar around the same time. Nobody saw them leave together, but they seem to remember them being going around the same time. When the cops picked him up, he couldn't explain where he was from around the time they figure the girl was killed. Said he didn't remember much from the time he left the bar until he woke up in his apartment. He lived in a student apartment on Twenty-First Street. His roommates couldn't say for sure that he'd been there."

"Did they have any physical evidence linking him to the scene?"

"Not a damn shred," she said. "They had fluids and some tissue samples, I think, but I don't think they ever introduced them at the trial. He was convicted on the witness statements and the lack of an alibi."

Damn, I thought. That's pretty slim evidence to execute a man on. No wonder she blew a fuse at the sentencing.

"I understand that you were a bit upset at your brother's sentencing. You threatened the judge?"

"Yeah, I lost it. I think I threatened to cut that bastard judge's balls off and stuff 'em down his throat." She laughed, but there was no humor in it.

"That's pretty serious. I'm surprised they didn't throw you in jail."

"Well, I was only fifteen at the time, so they took that into account. And, I'd just heard my only older brother sentenced to death. Henry and I were close. Until he got accepted into college, me and him and our mom lived in a little cracker box in Northeast over near the Navy Yard. After they put him in prison, I lived with my mom until I turned eighteen . . . same year I graduated high school. I joined the army. It was either that or take some minimum wage job waiting tables. I stayed in the army for two hitches, long enough to get my college degree, and got out last year. I was gonna take care of mama, but she died a week after I got out." She sniffled and wiped a tear from the corner of her eye. "Now, it's just me."

"You seem to have done well. I imagine the job here pays well?"

"It's not bad. The army trained me as a 68K, a medical lab specialist," she said. "That and my bachelor's degree got me a job as a lab assistant here, and if I play my cards right, I could become a section chief in a year or two."

"It seems that medicine runs in your

family."

"Hmph, I don't know," she said. "Well, maybe. Henry always talked about wanting to be a doctor, for as long as I can remember. I guess that's why I applied for lab specialist training when I enlisted."

She was much more relaxed now, though still with a sad look in her eyes whenever she mentioned her brother. All to be expected. Now, though, I had to move her into another area—one that she wasn't likely to be too happy about.

"Let's get back to the judge-"

"You mean that asshole, Carson? What about him?"

"Well, you threatened him in the courtroom."

"Yeah . . . I already told you that." Her brows came together, the ends curling up like little furry worms. "What's this all about?"

"I was just wondering whether or not you still harbored a grudge against Judge Carson?"

The brows sprang apart and arched upwards.

"He wouldn't be in my prayers at night, if that's what you mean."

"Not exactly," I said. "I mean, would you still be angry enough at him to threaten him, maybe . . . maybe even go a bit further?"

"I still think the bastard should burn in hell. But, I've grown up a lot since then. Why would I jeopardize my career by threatening a judge? They let me off before because I was just a kid, and my brother had just been sentenced to die. They might not be so lenient now."

TEN

There didn't seem to be much more I'd get from Yolanda Waylon, so I thanked her for her time, and prepared to go. She pressed me to tell her why I wanted to know if she'd threatened the judge. If she had done so, she already knew, and if not, it didn't seem to make a difference, so I confirmed that he'd received a threatening note.

I left her sitting there looking bemused. I didn't want to believe she was the person behind the threats. She'd already been through enough.

I drove back to the office. It was 4:15 when I got there. Heather was shuffling a stack of papers when I walked in.

"Didn't expect you back today," she said.

"Hey, I only leave early on Friday," I said. "Anyway, I didn't really get much out of Yolanda Waylon. She's an angry young woman, and with good reason, but I don't see her as the type to send anonymous notes. She seems more the in your face type."

"Hm, well, maybe Penelope Payton's the note type. I found an address for her of sorts. She runs a combination bookstore-coffee shop over near Howard University."

I looked at my watch. "It's getting late, maybe I'll check it out tomorrow. What's the address?"

She pulled out one of the sheets of paper she'd been shuffling. "It's at T and Ninth Street." She smiled. "You'll like this. The place is called 'The Witch's Brew.'"

I shrugged.

"It's near a college campus," I said. "I'd expect some crazy ass name. Did you find out anything else about her?"

"No, just that she opened the place about seven years ago. No criminal record. Nothing much on the web about her at all, actually, which is a bit strange in itself. Everyone has something about them on the Internet."

Heather has a hard time believing that anyone could live in the twenty-first century and not be all over cyberspace, as she calls it. I'm not so sure about it, though. She pulled out another one of the papers and studied it for a moment.

"One other thing," she continued. "The other names the judge gave you are a wash. One's got Alzheimer's and has been in a nursing home for the past six years, and the other's been in prison for four years. Of the names he gave you, those are the only ones involving the death penalty."

"That doesn't leave us much to go on," I said.

"Yeah, we don't even know for sure that the judge's been actually threatened."

I looked at her with a frown and raised eyebrows. "You mean that he might have faked this? What for? Besides, you're the one who convinced me to take the damned case in the first place."

"No, that's not what I meant." She raised her hands, waving the sheaf of papers around. "I mean, it could be someone just pulling his chain to see how he might react."

"Well, I might not like the guy, but when I talked to him, he was taking it seriously."

"You know," she said. "The Waylon case is at the center of all this."

"Yeah, I already figured that. So what about it?"

"Well, I was just wondering if anyone else connected with the case has been threatened."

Damn! The woman's a genius. I'm beginning to think that the reason she's so good with computers is that she's secretly one of those androids—a machine with human skin on the outside and a computer for a brain.

"Good thinking, honeybunch," I said, using the nickname that she hated, and would only put up with me using. "Make a list of all the people involved on the government side of the case, the prosecutor, lead investigator . . . you know the drill. I'll reach out to them and see if any of them have received threats."

She laid a finger on the tip of her nose. "If anyone has, we'll know this is serious, if not . . . well, we have something else entirely."

I headed for my office. "Look, get started on that list of names," I said. "Oh, and did you get anything on the note?"

"Give me a break, will you? You only gave it to me this morning. My . . . friend has to slot it in with her other work. She promised to get back to me by the end of the day tomorrow."

"Yeah, okay. Sorry. Look, while you're preparing that list, see if you can get a list of the jurors in the case. After all, they're the ones who found the kid guilty. If someone's pissed off about the case, they're likely to be pissed at them as well, don't you think?"

She was scribbling away in her notepad. "Prosecutor, detective, jurors . . . yeah, got it."

She propped the notebook next to her computer and began pecking away at the keys.

I went into my office.

While will often start a case by jumping in feet first as I'd done with this one, at some point I like to sit down and map out a strategy. It helps to focus my mind on the key elements of the case, and often points in directions I've overlooked while I'm busy snooping. I sat at my desk, took out a yellow legal pad and number two pencil and began with what I knew.

Threats against Judge Isaac Carson

1. Anonymous note (who wrote it?)
2. Subject suspects Yolanda Waylon
3. She's angry, but I don't think it's her
4. Is this even related to Waylon case?
5. Heather thinks it is related to the case
6. Who else would want to threaten Carson?
7. Anyone else in Waylon case being threatened?

If that doesn't sound like much to go on, that's because it isn't. Basically, I was just groping in the dark, hoping to snag something, anything, that would help make sense of the case.

I sat there for a long time, staring down at my notes, but it didn't do any good. No brilliant insights popped into my mind. So, I put the pencil down and sat back in the chair with my back erect and my hands on my knees, palms up with my thumbs and second fingers touching lightly. I then began breathing slowly, feeling the air as it flowed in and out through my nostrils. In a few seconds, my entire body was relaxed, and I entered a meditative state. I could hear my heart beating, could hear the hum of the building's air conditioning unit, and the rushing sound as it forced air through the vent ducts. At the same time, I could hear the slight buzzing sound that came from the electrical outlets.

I sat that way for thirty minutes. I still didn't get any great insights, but I felt more relaxed. I knew that was just my mind's way of letting me know that I needed more information. I had a busy Friday ahead of me.

ELEVEN

I got an early start the next morning, arriving at the office a 7:45 and beating Heather in for a change—even if only by five minutes.

I still didn't have a clue as to the identity of the author of the Carson threat note, but I'd thought of a new way to approach the case.

Heather and I had been focusing on the Waylon trial, but it had dawned on me that if I understand the whole crime better, I might get a better fix on who bore grudges about what. So, I decided to start my day by talking to the detective who'd been in charge of the investigation.

Allan Bavan, now retired from the Arlington County Police Department, had been the detective on duty the night of the crime, and had been assigned lead on the case. It took some doing, but Heather managed to find his address which was surprisingly near our office. After retirement, Bavan had taken his savings and bought a houseboat, which he kept moored in the marina off Water Street, just south of the Waterfront Metro Station. It was too close to bother driving, so I cut between the condos behind the office and walked the two blocks.

Bavan's boat was hard to miss, the 40 foot long Aqua Chalet, looked like a red, white, and blue fiberglass shoebox sitting on dark blue pontoons. It was moored, aft toward the dock, reached by a six-foot-wide wooden gangplank. The back end had a canopy attached to the roof covering an open area containing a round white plastic table with four matching chairs. The whole thing bobbed up and down from the ebb and flow of the river as other craft moved past. This didn't seem to bother the man sitting in one of the chairs, in profile to me as I approached the gang plank. He sat there with a bottle of Miller Lite in his hand. A metal washtub sat on the deck near his foot. Several bottle necks protruded over the rim.

I recognized Bavan from the description Heather had gotten through her research, which included a department photo from before his retirement. He'd been a big brute then, but since his retirement four years ago, he'd gotten bigger. His bald head, which seemed to sit on his shoulders without benefit of a neck, glistened with sweat. Broad shoulders strained against the tattered polo shirt. The bulge of belly that slopped over the waist of his faded jeans was a sign that he'd really been enjoying his beer since retiring. He wasn't wearing any shoes.

But, despite the increased waist line, he hadn't lost his cop's instincts. He put the beer on the table. "What can I do for you, friend?" he asked without looking my way.

"Pretty good peripheral vision," I said.

"Without it, I wouldn't be enjoying my retirement." He swung the chair around and glared at me. "You don't look like a civilian, but you don't smell like a cop. Whaddaya want?"

"My name's Al Pennyback. I'm working a case that I think you might be able to help me with. Mind if I come aboard?"

He shrugged and pointed at the empty chair. The boat pitched up several inches just as I stepped onto the deck, causing me to grab at the table to maintain my balance. He smiled. I sat down and showed him my ID. He glanced at it and then back at me.

"Okay, Pennyback," he said. "What can I do for you?"

"You worked a case about ten years ago in Arlington . . . Henry Waylon."

He wrinkled his brow in concentration. "Yeah . . . I remember that case. Some college boy raped and strangled a 15-year-old white girl."

It wasn't lost on me that he'd specifically identified the race of the victim, but not the assailant.

"Yes, that's the case. Waylon got the death sentence."

"Yeah, he had the bad luck to draw Carson, the hanging judge, for his trial."

"The hanging judge?"

"Isaac P. Carson, toughest fucking judge in Northern Virginia," he said. "Always gave the maximum sentence. In Waylon's case, unfortunately, the state asked for the death penalty and Carson gave it to 'em. You know what the 'P' stands for in his name?"

I shook my head.

"Parker . . . Isaac Parker Carson. He's supposed to be named after some old judge from the 1800s out in Oklahoma or someplace who was called The Hanging Judge. Carson lived up to his name, too. He's given out more death sentences in his career than any other judge on the bench."

Interesting information, but useless to my case.

"Back to the case," I said. "What can you tell me about it?"

"Not much to tell really. A guy out walking his dog early one morning found the girl's body under Key Bridge . . . well, the dog did. Slipped the leash and ran after it." He picked the beer up and took a long swallow. "Took us a while to identify the body, because she didn't have a driver's license on her. Turns out she was only fifteen, which was why."

"What led you to Waylon as a suspect?"

"We canvassed the area," he said. "At one of the bars, a waitress recognized the girl's description. Remembered her talking to this black kid. We ID'ed him from a credit card receipt."

"That's it—that's the evidence you used to get an arrest warrant?"

His brow furrowed again, his hand stopped halfway to his face.

"No, we didn't get a warrant right away. But, when I went over to his apartment in DC and talked to the kid, he couldn't remember where he went after leaving the bar, he had scrapes and scratches on his hands and knees. There were witnesses who remember him leaving the bar around the same time the girl did. Taken all together, it's pretty compelling circumstantial evidence, enough for a jury to convict him."

"Were there any other suspects?"

Now he was frowning at me. He slammed the bottle down on the table.

"I don't think I like where you're going with this, Pennyback," he said. "I did that investigation by the book."

"Was there anything that put Waylon at the scene where the girl's body was found?"

He blinked. "Uh, no, but he was seen talking to her in the bar."

"He was seen talking to her, or was it her talking to him?"

"What's the fucking difference? They were seen talking the night she was killed."

"You said he had scratches on his body . . . did he get tested to see if any of the girl's tissue or blood was on him?"

He blinked again. "I think . . . maybe . . . I don't know."

"I'll take that to mean it wasn't done," I said. "You tied him to the girl in the bar, and someone *thinking* they might have left together, and slam, bam, thank-you, ma'am, you had yourself the perfect suspect."

"Hey, he was convicted by a fucking jury of his peers, dammit, not by me!"

I laughed. "His peers . . . you're kidding right? How many young black men were on that jury? How many black people of any age for that matter?"

His eyes went wide, and he looked down at his feet.

"That's what I thought," I said. "Face it, Bavan, the kid was convicted because someone put him near a white girl who was later raped and strangled. Here you had this young black man with no clear alibi. No physical evidence, but what the hell, everyone knows what *they're* like. I imagine the prosecutor painted a pretty gruesome and graphic picture of young Henry Waylon."

"That wasn't my doing. I just did the investigation. Hell, the kid's probably still got a few more years of appeals. You know how the system works."

I stared at him with my mouth open. He didn't know.

"Don't you listen to the radio or read the papers?"

"Not if I can help it," he said. "I only leave this fucking boat when I need food or beer."

"Henry Waylon was executed two days ago."

"Oh, I didn't know."

"You know what else? The day after he was executed, this outfit that tries to exonerate wrongfully accused people, got the results of the tests on the DNA found at the scene. It cleared Waylon. They executed the wrong man."

I clenched my jaws tight, watching as his mouth gaped.

"You sure of that?"

"Pretty damned sure," I said.

"B-but-"

"But nothing, Bavan. You fucked up and got the wrong man, now two innocent people are dead."

He glared daggers at me, and made a growling sound deep in his throat.

"I just did my fucking job. Hell, even the kid's drinking buddies, who also happened to be his roommates, said they think him and the girl left at the same time, and they couldn't say what time he got back to his apartment."

He took another drink from the bottle. His hand was shaking.

"Look, this was probably just a seduction gone bad, you know," he said. There was a slight tremor in his voice. "We learned that the vic, Colleen Adamson, we found out that she was a bit of a wild one, you know. Always runnin' off and doing crazy things. Way I figure it, she was out carousing, and had a taste for some dark meat, but changed her mind at the last minute. They'd been drinkin', and maybe the kid just didn't wanta take no for an answer, and he squeezed too hard. You know, maybe he didn't really intend to kill her. Anyway, I did my fucking job on this case."

"Yeah, it was a hell of a job you did," I said. "Two innocent people are dead, and now someone's threatening the people responsible for one of those deaths. You just might find yourself on that list."

"Wha-"

"Oh, did I forget to tell you? Someone's making threats against Judge Carson for sentencing Waylon to death. They're very likely to want to come after the cop who arrested him." I stood. "That's the case I'm working on. Thanks for your help. If you get any threats, I can include you in my case . . . for five hundred a day plus expenses."

I left him sitting there with his mouth open.

TWELVE

As I walked back into the office, Heather looked up. She was smiling broadly.

"Hey, you're back," she said. "I have a long list of names for you. You want me to email them, or would you rather have them on paper?"

She knew the answer to that. I always prefer to holding paper in my hands. There's just something unreal about information on that little laptop screen. I growled at her and went into my office without responding to her question.

I sat down and pulled out my list, hoping that maybe if I stared at it long enough something would come to me. As I looked at it, I did think of a couple more things to add to it;

Threats against Judge Isaac Carson

1. Anonymous note (who wrote it?)
2. Subject suspects Yolanda Waylon
3. She's angry, but I don't think it's her
4. Is this even related to Waylon case?
5. Heather thinks it is related to the

case
6. Who else would want to threaten
   Carson?
7. Anyone else in Waylon case being
   threatened?
8. Were there any other suspects in the
   Rape/murder?
9. Detective investigating case was a
   total fuckhead (have Heather check
   Bavan!!!!

My list was getting longer, but I was no closer to an understanding of what was going on than I'd been at the start. Well, that's not completely true. I was pretty sure I knew that Allan Bavan had learned of Henry Waylon early in his investigation, and had probably not even looked any further for suspects. Of course, that still didn't explain how the prosecution had come up with enough circumstantial evidence to convince a jury to convict. Or, had I missed something?

I'm a puzzle freak. I cannot resist a good puzzle, and this case was becoming one big puzzle. Nothing was making sense. That's when I'm in my element. The chase was on! All I had to do was figure out who to chase.

Heather rapped lightly on my door and walked in carrying a single sheet of paper.

Before she could say anything, I blurted out, "Heather, I want you to dig up everything you can on retired detective Allan Bavan."

"Did you get a bad vibe from him?" she asked.

"Let's just say, talking to him generated more questions than answers." That, and I didn't like the guy.

"Okay, I'll get on it. In the meantime, I've

made a list of everyone I think might be related to this mess." She put the sheet of paper on my desk, smoothing it out.

It was a pretty long list of names, neatly typed, and as usual with Heather, she hadn't stopped at *just* names. The top two names, though, caught me by surprise:

Henry Waylon – convicted of rape/murder '92 (22), executed '02(32)
Colleen Adamson – rape/murder victim '92.(15)

As I looked at the two names, though, it began to make sense. After all, this whole thing started with these two people and a chance encounter in a bar. I scanned the rest of the list.

Henry Waylon – convicted of rape/murder '92 (22), executed '02(32)
Colleen Adamson – rape/murder victim '92.(15)
Malcolm Jenkins – Waylon's lawyer/public defender
Thomas Macauley – assistant DA/prosecutor
Isaac P. Carson – presiding judge
Allan Bavan – lead detective on Waylon's case
Yolanda Waylon – Henry's sister (25)
Penelope Payton – Henry's girlfriend (30)
Charles Armstrong – Henry's classmate/roommate (32)
Michael Fletcher – Henry's classmate/roommate (34)
Jurors:
Gunther Weiss – foreman, recently deceased (72)
Alison Morgan (50)
Lane Coltrane (60)
Joseph Leslie (68)
William Gordon (65)
Melvin Pettigrew (60)
Samuel Carter (61)
Edgar Melton (62)
Bettina Adams (60)
Lance Woodson (52)
Ben Johnson (67)
Raymond Harris (62)

After I reached the bottom of the list, I looked up at Heather. She stood there, smiling down at me like a doting mother watching her slow-to-learn child work his way through his first reading exercise unaided.

"Okay," I said. "It looks good. Real neatly done and all that. But, what am I supposed to do with it? And, I assume the numbers in brackets are ages, but what do they have to do with anything?"

Her eyebrows twitched and her lips formed a pout.

"Well, I just thought it would be useful to have a list of everyone who had anything to do with the case," she said. She stared down her nose at me. "Yeah, the numbers are ages. I started with Henry and Colleen because I was struck by how young they were. But, then, I thought it interesting that everyone on the jury was so much older than Henry. I mean, how could that be called a jury of his peers? The youngest person on that jury was nearly 20 years older than the defendant."

Of course, it made perfect sense when she explained it like that.

"What about the racial composition of the jury?" I asked. "I imagine it was all-white?"

"Uh, I didn't check that. Give me a few hours, though, and I'll have that information as well. Good thinking. I wonder if his defense attorney paid any attention to that?"

"He was a court-appointed public defender, so I doubt it," I said. "But, when I talk to him, I'll ask."

"Is he next on your list of people to talk to?"

"No, I think I need a bit more background. I haven't talked to Lucy in a while. She probably covered the case for the *Post*. I think I'll pick her brain and see what she remembers."

Lucy, Lucinda Garcia Mendez, was a features writer for *The Washington Post* who wrote under the byline Lucy Mendez. We met a decade ago when I was investigating the murder of Darion Watkins, one of Sandra's students. From that time, Lucy had been following my cases, and doing the occasional feature. It had been her who'd come up with the 'Brown Knight' nickname, which had stuck. We weren't what you might call best friends, but she we did each other the occasional favor.

I called her, and we arranged to meet at 11:00 at Freedom Plaza, a nice urban park on E Street, one block west of the *Washington Post* building. I promised to bring bagels and coffee.

THIRTEEN

Freedom Park is a nice place to eat lunch. With E Street to the north and Pennsylvania Avenue to the south, and sitting areas with nice shade trees at each end, it's a favorite place to eat lunch, rivaled only by Pershing Park to the west. But, Pershing Park's close to the White House, and under continuous scrutiny by the Secret Service.

I arrived at 10:50 and claimed a bench at the east end of the park, closest to Lucy's building. She arrived precisely at 11:00.

I saw her coming a half block away. Lucy Mendez is hard to miss, even in a crowd. She was brought to DC from Puerto Rico when she was six, and had grown up in the area. About five-four, she had medium sized, conical breasts that swayed when she walked, even when she was wearing a bra, and wide hips that betrayed the African side of her ancestry. Her skin was very light brown, which set off the golden brown of her eyes. Her jet black hair was cut short, framing her oval face. In the July heat, she was wearing a pair of hip hugging brown pants with a matching sleeveless blouse. A couple of guys, probably government employees from one of the nearby agencies, almost collided with the mailbox at the corner as she passed. The way one of them whipped his head around, I'd be surprised if he didn't experience some pain from whiplash.

Lucy is in her mid-thirties—I've never pried for her exact age—and, if I hadn't met Sandra before I met her, well, let's just say she's old enough for a 50-year-old geezer like me. As far as I could tell, she wasn't married, or even in a committed relationship. Lucy was married to the job.

As she came near, I saw that she was carrying a little notebook, and that she had a pen clipped to the belt of her pants.

I held up the brown bag containing the bagels and coffee.

"Hope you like sour cream and onions," I said as she plopped down on the bench next to me and crossed her legs.

"Sounds fine to me, but I hope you remembered to put lots of cream in the coffee." She opened the notebook, put it on her knee, and unclipped the pen.

"Hey, let's at least eat first. Besides, it'll be me asking the questions today. Oh, and I did remember the cream—two little containers, and three sugars."

"Okay, pass me the chow, and start asking your questions." She didn't, however, put her notebook away.

I watched as she extracted the bagel and one container of coffee, before passing the bag back to me. I took out the remaining bag and the container of black coffee I'd bought for myself. She took a healthy bite from the bagel, chewed it, and then washed it down with a swig of coffee.

"You know, you really shouldn't do that," I said. "Your food doesn't digest properly when you wash it down like that."

"Hmph," she said. "You eat your way, and I'll eat mine." She took another bit, repeated the chewing thing, and washed it down again, giving me a 'screw you' look.

"Don't say I didn't warn you."

"Are you gonna ask your damn questions, or spend my lunch hour trying to teach me how to eat?"

I know when to quit. "I'm working a case that's related to a trial that took place in Virginia about ten years ago," I said. "Kid named Henry Waylon was convicted of rape and murder."

She stopped eating. Her expression hardened.

"The Waylon case. I didn't cover it, but I remember it well."

"What can you tell me about it?"

"What's to tell? You know he was finally executed earlier this week."

"Yeah, I heard it on the news."

"Did you also hear that the day after he was executed, the Innocence Project got a lab result on DNA from the crime scene that indicates he was innocent?"

"Yeah, I heard that too," I said. "But, the news didn't say what it was that cleared him."

"They wouldn't. Not that it won't eventually get out, and when it does, the shit will hit the fan."

"What could be worse than the fact that they executed an innocent man?"

She held her coffee container up and stared at me over the Styrofoam lid. Her brown eyes twinkled like the star at the top of a holiday tree.

"I haven't had a chance to read the report myself," she said. "But, someone I know and trust has, and he said, the report shows that the DNA on Colleen Adamson was from a quote Caucasian male end quote."

It took a second for that to sink in.

"Whoa!" I said. "You mean the evidence showed that it was a white guy that raped that poor girl?"

"Oh, and that's not the half of it. My friend said he had it on good authority that the prosecutor knew this before going to trial, but they couldn't find a match to the DNA, and since the victim's family was well connected, and the community was up in arms about the whole thing, they went ahead and stuck it to Henry Waylon."

"You're not kidding when you say the shit'll hit the fan if . . . when this gets out. Man, the activists who've been complaining about racial profiling will go ape shit when they get wind of this. Are you sure about that part about the prosecutor?"

"Come on, Al," she said. "Does a bear shit in the woods? There's no way he couldn't have known."

"What about the cops investigating the case? Could they have known?"

"It's a damn good possibility."

"I've heard of prosecutors and the cops walking close to the line in order to get a conviction," I said. "But, this is misconduct on a grand scale."

"Yeah, I'm working a piece on

prosecutorial misconduct right now, and I think this is going to be central to my story."

I was floored. I'm no fan of racial profiling, but I could understand how cops working inner city beats could fall into that trap. I could also see a prosecutor pushing the limits to get a conviction if he thought the prisoner was guilty but might get off on a technicality. But, to knowingly withhold evidence and convict an innocent man—I found that hard to get my mind around. I was thinking I might pay another call on retired detective Bavan. I'd also be calling on the prosecutor.

"So, Lucy, what else can you tell me about this case?"

"Not much that that ferret Heather can't dig out. Oh, there was rumbling at the time of the trial that the DA was pressing so hard to convict because the victim was white and Waylon was black. Whether or not it's true is open to question, but the black community on both side of the Potomac at the time were in a mood to believe it. Imagine how they'll react when they find out what was really done back then."

"You don't think there could be racial incidents in this day and age to you?"

"Hey, pal, people thought the city was pretty quiet back then," she said. "But, don't forget, just the year before there'd been an outbreak of violence between the Latino community and the police here in the District—over in Mount Pleasant. There were even a few protests here that got out of hand after the Rodney King beating in L.A. in 1992. I hate to say it, my friend, but this area is often just one incident away from riots."

"So, I imagine the official position on this is to try and sweep it under the rug?"

"Sure, they'd love to do that, but the cat's already out of the bag. They're gonna have to do some major league damage control on this one."

Lucy Mendez is one of the few people I know who can hold a conversation and eat at the same time. While we'd been talking, she'd demolished her bagel and finished all but a few sips of her coffee, while I was still sitting there holding three-quarters of a bagel and over half a cup of now lukewarm coffee. After what she'd said, though, I'd lost most of my appetite anyway.

"Okay," I said. "So the prosecutor's dirty, probably the lead investigator as well . . . what about the judge?"

"Old Isaac P. 'Hanging Judge' Carson? Naw, he's squeaky clean. Not that some of the shit's not gonna slop over on him when this really hits, but I doubt he knew about the withholding of evidence, or that he'd have allowed it if he'd known. Carson was one of the first black jurists to rise to a senior position in the Virginia court system, and he did it by being a strict interpreter of the law. Also, in a state that leans way to the right on law and order issues, he had to be pretty strict to keep the wolves at bay. Now, I've answered your questions, how 'bout you answer one for me?"

"I will if I can."

"What case are you working on?"

Lucy's always been up front with me. I saw no harm in telling her what I was working on, as long as I protected my client's privacy. "Someone connected with the

Waylon case has received a threatening letter, and I'm trying to find out who's behind the threat."

She smiled. For some reason, it made me think of a coyote about to close in on an unsuspecting rabbit.

"So, someone's threatening the judge?"

"You know bloody well I can't divulge the name of my client without express permission."

"It *is* the judge." She smiled in anticipation, I knew, of the headline that would go with that story.

"Look, Lucy," I said. "I will neither confirm nor deny, but I am asking that you not publish anything . . . at least for now."

She pouted at me.

"Oh, you're no fun. Of course I won't publish anything until you tell me it's okay to run with it," she said. "But, I get the exclusive, right?"

"Fair enough."

I knew I wouldn't get any better deal than that. It was certainly better than the deal Henry Waylon got.

FOURTEEN

Back at the office, I told Heather what I'd learned from Lucy. This, along with my conversations with Carson and Bavan, went into the case file, which she kept on her computer, with a copy backed up to a CD that she kept locked in her file cabinet. I still had a few hours left in the week, so we went over the list to see who else I could talk to. Charles Armstrong and Michael Fletcher, who had been Henry Waylon's classmates and had shared an apartment with him, had completed their medical training and were both doctors working at a free clinic on 10th Street, Southeast, near Eastern Market.

Figuring to get two interviews in one visit, and then go home and get ready for the weekend, I drove over. I found a place to park a few blocks away on D Street, and walked back to the clinic, arriving at 3:35.

The 10th Street Clinic, as the sign over the glass double doors proclaimed, was a derelict one-story building in a block of derelict buildings. The sidewalk, its uneven slabs pockmarked with potholes and cracks, was littered with yellowed and crumpled paper, crushed beer cans, and the broken necks of liquor bottles. At first glance, you would have thought the derelict buildings were abandoned, but they were not. To the left of the clinic was a beauty shop, and to its right was a rib joint. The three buildings together emitted a strange concoction of odors; peroxide, formaldehyde, and barbecue sauce. At first it stung the nose, but after a few breaths, was actually comforting.

The clinic had once been some kind of store if the glass display windows to either side of the doors were any indication. Now, the windows were covered with notices and graffiti, and the display shelves only held dust.

Inside, there was a reception desk to the right, manned by a thin woman with dark chocolate skin, light brown eyes, and short black hair done in tight cornrows from the front to the back of her head. She wore light green scrubs that failed to hide the fact that she wore no bra, not that her tiny breasts needed one. 'Yvonne' was sewn into the left breast pocket of her scrubs. To the left were six rows of plastic chairs, each row containing five chairs. The first two rows were occupied with patients either waiting to give their information to the receptionist or to be seen by a nurse or doctor. As I approached the reception desk, a Hispanic looking woman wearing light green scrubs, with a stethoscope around her neck, came through a door in the back of the room. "Ms. Johnson," she called. In the front row, an obese woman with her arm in a sling stood. "This way please, Ms. Johnson, the doctor will see you now." The nurse, with a solicitous smile, held the door until the fat woman had waddled through, then she pulled it shut.

The receptionist looked up at me with a tired smile when I stopped in front of the desk.

"What's the problem?" she asked. Her tone said she'd asked that question a thousand times. She held a pen poised over a pad of forms on the desk.

I flashed my ID. "I'd like to speak with Michael Fletcher or Charles Armstrong," I said. "It's regarding a case I'm working on, and it's very important."

The tired smile was replaced by a momentary look of confusion, which was as quickly replaced by a raised eyebrow look of interest. She took a quick glance at a clipboard hanging on the wall behind her.

"Uh, sorry, but Dr. Fletcher's not on until the late shift," she said. "He'll be in around ten. Dr. Armstrong's here, but he's probably with a patient now."

"Well, could I speak to Armstrong, then?"

"Okay, have a seat over there." She pointed to the rows of chairs. "I'll see when he's available."

As I turned toward the chairs, she lifted the phone receiver and spoke into it in hushed tones.

I walked past the two occupied rows of chairs, mostly black women, a couple with sniffling kids, but I noticed two Hispanic looking men in the second row. This part of the District is overwhelmingly black, but lately I've noticed more and more Hispanics around the city. Slowly, with the upheavals in Central and South America, the racial demographics of Washington have been changing, with Hispanics on track to eventually become the largest ethnic group if their rate of growth continues. It started with Salvadorians fleeing the fighting between the Sandinistas and the Contras, and was soon joined by flows from Peru, Venezuela, Colombia, and many other countries. Unlike Mexicans, who tend to stop in the border states where they often have relatives, or where they can get jobs in agriculture or construction, the new immigrants from the south move toward the nation's capital where they can have access to our politicians, as many seek help to settle the mess in their home countries.

I moved to the fourth row, keeping an empty row of seats between me and the waiting patients, a couple of whom coughed every few minutes. Hospitals are the most common place to catch a bug, and I had no idea what microbes the ten people in front of me were sharing. I sat in the chair closest to the back wall and waited.

After about fifteen minutes, the door through which the nurse had vanished opened again. A man, wearing scrubs that were a darker green than the receptionist or nurse, with dark stains on the knees and near the waist, stepped out into the reception area. He had curly black hair that flopped over his ears and down over his forehead, stopping just short of bushy brows. His skin had the sun-bronzed olive complexion of a native of the Mediterranean region, but his eyes were dark blue. He was slight of build, and short—about five-seven or eight—and had the shy demeanor of the kid who is always picked last in playground games.

He looked at the receptionist, who pointed at me. I was pretty hard to miss, seated apart from the rest of the crowd as I was. I think, too, I was probably the only person seated there who didn't look like he needed to see a doctor.

He walked over to where I sat.

"You wanted to talk to me?" he asked.

I showed him my ID.

"Yeah, name's Al Pennyback," I said. "I'm a private investigator. You got a few minutes and a place we could talk in private?"

"Might I ask what this is about?"

I looked past him. The fat lady and one of the Hispanic men had turned in their chairs and leaned back.

"I'd really rather tell you that in private," I said, inclining my head in their direction. Both of them jerked back around, but that only caused the people sitting near them to turn to look at us.

He looked at them, and frowned.

"Okay," he said. "There's an exam room in back that's not in use right now. Come with me."

He turned and headed for the door. I rose and followed.

The reception area had been relatively quiet, with an occasional cough and the low hum of conversations. The area behind the wall, after he'd closed the door, was as quiet as a public library with a stern librarian. We walked past three doors. They were closed, but I could see movement through the milky glass panes in the top half. At the fourth door, he opened it and walked in, flipping on a light switch. The room, about half as large as my office—which is to say, just larger than a good-sized closet—was flooded with light from a large, circular overhead fixture, beneath which was a metal exam table. Off to the right were a stainless wash basin and a small mirror. Next to that was a glass covered cabinet containing several vials and bottles. The cabinet was secured with a large padlock. There was a small desk beneath the cabinet, and two straight back chairs. He took one and motioned me toward the other.

"Okay," he said when we were seated. "Why does a private investigator want to talk to me?"

"You shared an apartment with Henry Waylon, isn't that right?"

I asked the question bluntly for a reason. I wanted to see how he'd react to having Waylon's name just dropped on him like that. He reacted, all right. His face turned pale, and his mouth opened and closed like a fish struggling for air.

"W-why do y-you want to know?"

"I'm working on a case that involves Waylon's . . . situation," I said. "That's all I can tell you right now. But, I'm talking to everyone who knew him."

He stared at me, through me, for a long time. Then, his shoulders slumped and he sighed.

"Yes, Henry and I were roommates, along with Mike; that's Michael Meredith."

"Did you all get along? Were you close?"

"Yeah, uh, Henry and I were real close . . . Mike, not so much. He was more concerned with his grades. Not that Henry and I didn't do well. In fact, Henry was a freaking genius. He could read a book and regurgitate its contents almost verbatim. Good grades came easy to him. He helped me. Mike had to work harder, you know."

"Are you saying there were hard feelings between them because of grades?"

"No, that's not what I'm saying," he said. "Mike was just . . . so competitive, you know. Sometimes . . . I think he might have resented it a bit . . . Henry getting good grades so easy, you know. But, they got along. Everyone liked Henry."

"The night of the . . . incident . . . what do you remember?"

His face screwed up in a painful expression, and his lips trembled. It looked like he was going to cry.

"That's okay," I said. "Take your time. I know it must be tough to think about it."

"Tough? You don't know the half of it." A tear slid from the corner of his left eye. "Henry was like a brother to me . . . like the brother I never had. I was an only child, and my parents died when I was in my last year of high school."

He leaned forward in the chair, hugging himself. As he talked, a bit of color had come back into his face.

"Let's focus on that night, okay," I said. "Where you went, who you talked to, what you did."

"Uh, yeah, sure. It was late May, right after finals," he said. "Henry, as usual, had aced them, but Mike and I hadn't done too bad either, so we decided to go out and celebrate. We started out at a couple of the pubs in Georgetown, on M Street, but then decided to walk over to Rosslyn. I don't even remember the name of the dive we were in . . . it was off Wilson Avenue."

"It was just the three of you?"

"Yeah. Henry's girlfriend, Penny, Penelope Payton . . . she was pre-med too . . . she'd sometimes go out with us, but one of her sorority sisters was sick, so she stayed in with her. Penny stayed in one of the sorority houses up on Twenty-Third Street. Anyway, it was just the three of us."

He shook himself, as if he was rousing from a dream.

"Tell me about the bar you went to in Virginia," I said. I kept my voice gentle, sensing that the memory was disturbing to him.

"It was just a bar, you know . . . dim lights, loud conversation, louder music. Mike and I were already a little buzzed by the time we arrived. Not Henry, though. He was always the responsible one when we went out."

"Some of the news reports I read hinted that he might have been drunk, and that's why he did what they say he did."

"Bullshit!" His eyes blazed briefly with anger. "I've never seen Henry drunk, and I shared an apartment with him for three years. Like I said, when we went out he was always the responsible one."

"Okay, got it. Who did you guys talk to in that bar?"

He cocked his head to the side, looking up at the peeling squares of soundproofing tile in the ceiling.

"At first, nobody," he said. "Then, this chick, a real hot blonde, came up to us. She really zoomed in on Henry, you know. Hey, the guy was pretty good looking. He worked out, and was a good athlete. Hell, every chick on campus had the hots for him."

"This hot blonde, was this the . . . was this Colleen Adamson?"

"Yeah. The one they say he raped and killed." He caught his breath and closed his eyes. When he opened them, tears spilled from both and coursed down his cheeks. "Man, I can't believe he's gone, you know. I mean, they executed him, and he didn't do it. I *know* he didn't do it."

"How do you know?"

Again, I kept my voice low and gentle, trying to get information from him without leading him. I wanted him to spill what was in his mind in as pure and unedited a form as possible.

"It just wasn't like him," he said. "Henry was kind and gentle, and he certainly didn't need to force women. If anything, he had to fight them off. Besides, he said he wasn't feeling well, and he did look a little green around the gills, you know. It was right after Mike had bought a round. Henry had just rebuffed this chick's . . . Colleen's . . . advances for the umpteenth time, telling her he already had a girlfriend, and he said he felt like he was gonna barf, you know, so he excused himself."

"What happened after that?"

He looked puzzled.

"I don't know," he said. "I . . . he didn't come back. After a while, the blonde . . . Colleen . . . wandered off too. Like I said, I was pretty buzzed at the time, and I guess I didn't pay any attention, but the next time I saw Henry was the next day. It was Saturday, and we were sleeping in. The cops came around noon and were knocking on our door.

I opened it, and they asked to speak with him. I was still a bit out of it, so I showed them to his room. He was sprawled across his bed, still dressed, and he'd puked on the floor. Well, they woke him up and took him away, to ask him a few questions, they said. Next thing I know, later that day, they formally charged him and he was thrown in jail."

"Wait a minute," I said. "You guys lived in DC, and the crime was committed across the river. Who came to the apartment to arrest Henry?"

"Well, there were two campus cops and a couple of uniformed Metro DC cops, and this beefy bald guy in a rumpled suit who didn't identify himself. I found out later he was an Arlington County detective, and that he was in charge of the investigation—his name's Bevin . . . no, Bavan."

"Did he interview you and your other roommate, Mike?"

His expression closed up. He looked from me to a spot on the floor a few inches in front of his feet. His fingers tapped soundlessly on the metal desk that sat between us.

"Yeah, but not until a few days later, the following Tuesday, I think. He wanted to know what we knew about Henry's movements on Saturday night, you know. Problem is, when we finally got home around two in the morning, we were both so wasted, we went straight to our rooms and didn't check if Henry was there."

"So, you have no idea where he was from the last time you saw him in the bar until the cops came the next day."

"I couldn't swear under oath that he went

straight back to the apartment from that bar," he said. "But, that's what he said he did, and I believe him."

"Apparently, the jury didn't. They convicted him."

He clenched his fists and pressed his lips tight until they were pale.

"That fucking jury didn't convict him because they thought he was guilty," he said. His voice was as tight as his clinched fists. "That bunch of bigoted bastards convicted him because he was a good looking black man with a white girlfriend, and someone had accused him of taking liberties with another white girl."

I leaned forward.

"You want to explain that?"

He took a deep breath.

"First, the jury was all white, you know, and mostly male. And then, Penelope, who is pretty white bread, testified for him, and I hear she broke down on the stand, professing her love and all, and crying that 'her Henry' could never hurt anyone. That had to go down hard with that bunch of dried up old white dudes. Hell, even if I'd sworn he was in the apartment all night, I think they would have still found him guilty."

"Are you sure he wasn't guilty?"

He looked like a semi-deflated blow-up doll. There was no longer even any anger in his eyes as he looked at me. Something else that I couldn't quite put a name to, but not anger. Guilt maybe? But, guilt about what?

"Yeah, I'm sure," he said. "And, you know . . . it was all my fault. Henry didn't even want to go out that night, but I talked him into it. If I'd left him alone, my best friend wouldn't be dead."

He dropped his head on his forearm. His shoulders shook as he silently cried. I stood and put a hand on his shoulder.

"It won't bring your friend back," I said. "But, I'm gonna try and determine the truth, so at least his good name will be restored."

He looked up at me, his eyes glistening, but merely nodded. I left him there as I made my way back to reception and then outside and to my car.

Catching the person who had committed the crime for which Henry Waylon was wrongfully executed wasn't the case I'd been hired to solve. But, it was now the case I was working on.

FIFTEEN

On Saturday, Sandra and I woke early, did our run and exercise, and had dry toast and coffee for breakfast. We were having a barbecue lunch at Buster's place, and Buster would be offended if we didn't arrive with good appetites. Buster Mayweather and I have been friends since the night he accompanied me to a morgue in Arlington to identify the mangled bodies of my wife and son. He'd sat with me at the morgue, and again back at my house, silent, but reassuring as I worked through my grief. A bear of a man, he'd been a star football player at the University of Maryland, on track to be drafted into the NFL until he blew out his knee in his senior year. Unable to play pro football, he'd joined the DC Metro Police Department, where he worked some of the toughest neighborhoods in the city, eventually being promoted to senior detective in the Homicide Division, specializing in street gangs who accounted for a large percentage of the area's homicides.

Buster, his wife Alma, a petite woman with an iron will, and his children, the twins,

Albert and Sandra, lived in a two-story brick house in the Northeast Quadrant of the District, in a neighborhood that was solidly middle class, with modest sized lawns, one and two-car garages, and fenced-in backyards. Buster had a two-car garage, in which he kept his car of the moment—currently a Dodge Charger—along with his wife's more sensible Honda Civic. His fenced-in backyard, just off a screened-in back porch, was divided into two sections; off to the left, under a towering oak tree, a sandbox, swing, and seesaw for the twins, and to the right, a wooden picnic table and brick grill for papa. When the weather was nice, Buster liked nothing better than holding court in his backyard as he thrilled us with the barbecue recipes he'd gotten from his great uncle, a North Carolina farmer who'd moved north, settling in Howard County, Maryland in the late forties.

When we arrived, the rest of our circle of friends was already there. Heather, in a pink polo shirt and mid-thigh shorts; Quincy, looking formal even in an open neck beige shirt and gray slacks; and Carlton 'Blood' Raine, in a black and red plaid shirt—with long sleeves despite the weather—and khaki pants with a sharp military crease—with Elizabeth Sung, his inseparable companion, on his arm. Elizabeth looked stunning in a lime green sundress that ended midway down a marvelous pair of thighs and displayed a generous amount of bronzed cleavage. Buster stood over his grill, dressed in a sleeveless black muscle shirt and faded jeans, over which was a knee-length white and red barbecue apron, with 'Honk if you

Love BBQ!' stitched across his broad chest. His bald head glistened with sweat, which flowed down his face to be collected by the neat goatee he now wore. Alma, whose head didn't even reach her six-foot-two husband's shoulders, wore a simple yellow summer frock that showed off her cocoa colored skin to perfection. The twins were in matching jumpsuits, with matching grass and dirt stains. They waved at us from the sandbox, but since we weren't obviously carrying gifts for them, otherwise ignored our arrival.

Sandra and I wore nearly matching ensembles. I had on a black polo shirt with black cotton cargo pants, and she wore a black scoop-necked blouse with black mid-thigh shorts.

I was carrying a bottle of Stolichnaya vodka and a five-pound package of Polish sausage, while Sandra had a bottle of red wine and two packages for the twins. We gave the food and drink to Alma, who put the drinks on the table and handed the sausage to Buster. He immediately tore the wrapping off the sausage and dumped them onto the grill next to the ribs that were nearly cooked.

"Sausage and ribs washed down with Stoli," he said. "All we need is corn on the cob, and we are good to go."

Quincy and Carlton moved over toward us, both eying the vodka.

"Help yourselves," Buster said. "And, make me a vodka tonic while you're at it." He turned back to me. "What up, bro? What kinda trouble you makin' these days?"

Before I could answer him, Sandra held the remaining two packages up. "I have a package here for someone named Albert, and another one for someone named Sandra," she said. "Anyone here by that name?"

The twins' heads popped up and their gaze fixed on Sandra like lasers—or, more accurately, upon the packages she held aloft. In an explosion of sound, color and motion, they erupted from the sandbox and swarmed her.

"Auntie Sandra, Auntie Sandra," they shouted in unison. "What'd you bring us?"

"Something I think you'll like." She handed each of them a package.

The wrappings were turned into confetti in a blur of motion, revealing two of those hard cover pop-up books where the little figures that illustrate the story pop up as you turn the page.

Buster and Alma encourage them to read, and always read to them, and usually when Sandra and I buy them gifts, except at Christmas, it's books. They jumped up and down, shouting gleefully, for a few seconds, and then scooted off to sit on the steps to check out their new acquisitions.

"Man," Buster said. "I don't know where them two get the energy. I get tired just watching 'em. Now, bro, back to you. What you up to these days?"

Three pairs of eyes looked expectantly at me. If there's anyone other than Sandra and Heather I'm willing to share case information with, it's these three, so I told them what I was working on, including the information I'd obtained from Lucy. When I finished, they were all shaking their heads and frowning.

"Do you think Lucy's information about the prosecution withholding information is credible?" Carlton asked.

Before I could answer, Buster slammed the large fork he was holding against the grill.

"Hell, they do it a lot," he said. "But, this is the first time I've ever heard of it being done in a capital case."

"Such an action is completely unethical," Quincy said. "It's grounds for disbarment at a minimum and possible criminal action as well."

"In most cases it would be grounds for the verdict being overturned," Buster said. "Ain't gonna do the accused much good in this case, though."

Carlton had been listening quietly, the expression on his lean brown face unreadable. When he spoke, his voice was so quiet, I had to lean in to hear him clearly. "Do you think whoever's behind the threats against the judge knows about this?"

That hadn't occurred to me, but if that was the case, the list of potential targets just grew.

"I don't know," I said. "I've been working on the assumption that whoever's doing this was just pissed that an innocent man had been wrongfully executed. If what was done is known, and if the *Post* knows it, there's every possibility that someone else does as well, it puts a whole new light on the case."

"And, the judge doesn't want to go to the authorities?" Buster asked. "Seems to me that'd be the smart thing to do."

"It's politics," Quincy said. "I know Judge Carson. He's being considered for a seat on the federal court. If this goes public, especially the illegal actions of the ADA who prosecuted the case, it could sabotage his candidacy."

"Even if he was unaware of what was done?" I asked, knowing what the answer would be.

"It doesn't matter," Quincy said. "He'd be tainted by it. It happened in his courtroom. He's having enough trouble with the news that DNA evidence points to the kid's innocence, but in today's law and order age, especially the paranoia that's gripped this country since 9/11, he might be able to overcome that. After all, it was the jury that found the kid guilty; he only applied the sentence provided for by the law. But, prosecutorial misconduct—that will taint everyone connected with the case."

"Which reminds me," I said, turning to Buster. "Do you think the cop in charge of the investigation might have been in on withholding evidence?"

He screwed up his eyes, frowning at me. Buster's a cop, and his gut reaction is to defend other cops, but, he's also a straight shooter who hates dirty cops—and, he's my friend. He knew I wouldn't ask the question if I didn't have good reason.

"Well, it's the crime scene techs who process the information, and they send it to the DA's office, but usually, they also share it with the cop in charge of the case. It helps prepare him if he has to testify."

"So, if I'm hearing you right, it's unlikely the Arlington cops were unaware of the evidence that would have cleared Waylon?"

He nodded slowly. His expression was pained.

"Okay," I said. "Do you know an Arlington detective named Allan Bavan" He's retired now, but he was the lead detective on the case ten years ago."

His lips curled down, and his eyes blazed.

"Yeah, I know that son of a bitch," he said. "I know him well. I've had to work with him a couple of times, back when I was new on the force and we had cases that overlapped jurisdictions. What do you want to know about him?"

"Everything you can remember."

He remembered a lot.

Allan Bavan was a junior detective when Buster first met him. He'd originally worked for the DC Metropolitan Police Department, but as that department began hiring more black, Hispanic, and Asian officers, Bavan had refused to be partnered with any of the minority officers. He'd also been disciplined on several occasions for excessive force during arrests of non-white suspects. He'd finally quit the DC police force and applied for a job with the Arlington County Police Department. Buster, a newly promoted junior detective by now with the DC force, had first encountered Bavan during the investigation of a gun smuggling case involving dealers from the District buying guns from Virginia gun shops and bringing them back across the Potomac, where they more often than not ended up figuring in some of the DC's most vicious crimes.

The first time Buster had to work with the man, he'd refused to share information, refused even to shake his hand. He'd never say anything directly, but Buster had gotten the distinct that it was his race Bavan objected to, because he was often chummy with white detectives from DC. In conversations with a few of the black officers working in Arlington, Buster had learned that Bavan also refused to work with them, preferring to work alone instead. He continued in Arlington to be particularly harsh whenever dealing with black, Hispanic, or Asian suspects, but with the increase in Asian gang activity, his superiors chose to turn their heads at his actions.

"So," he said as he came to the end of his story. "My guess is that when Bavan learned of a black suspect in that rape case, he stopped looking at any other possibility."

"You're saying he knew Waylon was innocent?" I asked.

"No, I'm saying he didn't give a damn," Buster said, his voice barely above a whisper. "He had a good suspect, and he didn't look to see if there might be someone else. If you're saying evidence pointed to a white perp, he just might have gone along with keeping it under wraps."

"The problem will be proving that," Quincy said.

Leave it to good old Quince to point out the obvious. But, he was right.

"So, young fella, what do you plan to do now?" Carlton asked.

"Well, I've been hired to find out who's threatening the judge, but I think I'll also try and find out who raped and killed that girl."

Buster chuckled.

"Why am I not surprised at that?" he said. "Hey, ribs are ready. Who wants one?"

"Me, me," yelled the twins in unison, dropping their books beside the steps and racing over.

SIXTEEN

I arrived at the office at a quarter to eight on Monday, thinking I'd break a record and beat Heather yet again, only to find her hunched over her computer staring at the screen.

"What's got you so interested so early in the morning?" I asked.

Her head jerked upwards and her chair slid back until it bumped the book case behind her desk.

"Don't do that. You scared me."

"Sorry, I thought you heard the door opening. What's so fascinating?"

She turned her laptop around so that I could see the screen.

"I was just reading the morning paper," she said. Most people actually *read* a newspaper. Heather gets her news via computer. "I just happened to see this obituary notice in the local section of the *Post* online."

I leaned forward for a closer look.

Joseph Leslie, Korean War Vet, Dies

Joseph Leslie, age 68, who was a 16-year-old Marine during the Korean War, and who participated in McArthur's famous Inchon Landing, died yesterday at his home in Arlington.

Leslie, who had been ill for some time, had been living in the Brentwood Assisted Living facility on Fairfax Drive in Arlington, is said to have died from a massive heart attack, according to senior medical staff at the facility. He is survived by a cousin, Malcolm Leslie of Warrenton, Va. A memorial service will be held on Thursday, July 25 at the Brentwood chapel.

Leslie will be interred at Arlington National Cemetery.

.

"You're a bit young to be paying attention to obits, aren't you?" I asked.

"You don't recognize the name, do you?"

"Should I?"

She gave me a look of exasperation. "I don't know why I even bother making lists for you. Mr. Leslie was one of the jurors in the Waylon case."

"Oh." What else could I say? I'm not that good with names, and I'd only seen his name on a long list of names, and not near the top of the list at that.

"Don't you think it rather strange, two jurors on the same case dying so close together, and of heart attacks?"

I shrugged.

"The guy was 68, and he had a bad ticker," I said. "Same thing with the other one, and he was even older."

She shrugged and pulled her computer back around.

"I seem to remember a certain private investigator once saying to me that there's no such thing as coincidence."

"Look here, young lady, don't you go using my words against me like that." I waggled a finger in her face. "So, two old guys with heart conditions croak from heart attacks. That happens every day. So, they just happen to have served on the same jury. So what? That's not the kind of coincidence I was talking about, that's more in the category of 'shit happens.' Besides, unless our mystery person can somehow work magic, I don't see how he . . . or she can induce heart attacks."

She had the decency to look chastened.

"Okay, okay, you have a point. It just struck me as odd is all. I mean, we just happen to be working this case, and all of a sudden two people related to it drop dead. Don't you think that odd?"

"Odd as in freaky how the world works, yeah," I said. "But, odd in is it somehow related to the threats against our client, no. Now, what do you have that actually relates to the case?"

She picked up a single sheet of paper.

"My friend faxed me the report on the note," she said. "She'll send the note itself back later today."

I looked over her shoulder. The first sentence had at least two words of three syllables each and what appeared to be Greek or Latin, or some other language I didn't recognize.

"Why don't you summarize it for me," I

said.

She held it up close to her face and peered at it for a few seconds. Then, she put it down.

"Well, in essence, it says that the paper was a common bond printer paper like the kind you can buy in any office supply store. If they had the box it came from, they could compare it, but with just one sheet, they can't tell you where it came from." She traced down the page with her finger. "The print on the paper was from a laser printer, but again, they can only verify what printer if they had it to compare. They do say, it's a Hewlett-Packard printer, similar to the kinds you find in public libraries or those stores that offer print services. If they had the printer they could compare and confirm that it was the one used. The writing style doesn't match anyone in the FBI data base, and doesn't really give any clues to the writer's frame of mind." She hesitated at the bottom of the page. "There were fingerprints on the paper, thumbprints on the front and a few fingers on the backside that matched Isaac P. Carson, so no surprise there. No other prints were found. Oh, and they found minute traces of talc embedded in the paper fiber, indicating that whoever handled it probably wore some kind of surgical glove, but you can buy those off the shelf in many drug stores or medical supply stores, and there's no way of tracking all the purchases of rubber gloves in this area – provided they were even purchased in this area."

She stopped, put the paper down, and looked up at me.

"In other words," I said. "If we find out

where it was written, and who wrote it, they can verify it for us."

"Uh, when you put it that way, it does sound a bit useless, doesn't it?"

"You think? Okay, so it means we have to depend on your ability to coax information out of people and computers, and my charm and skill on the streets."

"Well, I do agree that you're skilled at what you do," she said.

I started to turn away when her words hit me. I turned back. "Are you applying that I'm not charming?"

She looked up, all innocent looking and smiling.

"Aw, you're charming enough when it comes to women . . . they all seem to have the hots for you . . . well, most of them anyway. But, when you're hot on a case, you can be pretty intimidating."

"But, that's part of my charm don't you know."

SEVENTEEN

Even though I'd decided to try and solve the ten-year-old murder case, I had to keep in mind that Isaac Carson was paying me to find out who was sending him threats. I'd been giving it thought over the weekend, and had come to the conclusion that it had to be someone close to Henry Waylon. I'd only talked to two people, his sister, Yolanda, and his former roommate, Charles Armstrong. Yolanda had every reason to be angry at what had happened to her brother, but I was having a hard time seeing her as the type to send anonymous threats—or any threats at all for that matter—and, Armstrong didn't strike me as the type to get involved in any kind of confrontation.

In other words, neither of them, in my opinion, were viable suspects. That only left two people; Penelope Payton, the former girlfriend, and his other roommate, Michael Fletcher. Heather still hadn't gotten a home address for Payton, and I knew that sooner or later I could catch Fletcher at the free clinic, so I decided to visit Payton at her place of business.

I debated calling ahead, but thought it might be better to just drop in. That way, she wouldn't have time to prepare answers to my questions.

Before leaving the office, I asked Heather to get contact information for Thomas Clayton, the ADA who'd prosecuted the case, and Malcolm Jenkins, the public defender who'd represented Waylon, and see if she could set up appointments with them.

I wanted to talk to Payton and Fletcher to see if either of them might be capable of making threats, but the two lawyers were part of my personal investigation.

The Witch's Brew was in Northwest DC, between Seventh and Eighth Streets just off Florida Avenue. It was a two-story brick building, painted a light shade of purple—almost blue—with pink trim at the corners, and beige trimmings on the large windows on the ground floor to either side of the entrance and on the four windows on the second floor. The roof was steeply pitched and covered with black slate. Little gray stone gargoyles sat on the corners leering down at the sidewalk. It shared a wall with the buildings on either side. The one of the left was three floors, and was made of red stones interspersed with black, and housed a dance studio. On the right, another two-story building of white brick, had signs for a barber shop on the ground floor and a dressmaker on the top floor.

The absence of a visible access to the second floor of the Witch's Brew gave me the sense that the second floor of the building was probably where Penelope Payton lived, which explained why Heather hadn't been able to find her residence address. Her business and residence were one and the same.

I found an empty parking slot on a diagonal street around the corner from the building, put an hour's worth of quarters into the parking meter and walked back.

A small brass bell over the door tinkled as I pushed into the place.

I'd been picturing in my mind what a place called 'Witch's Brew' would look like, and it halfway lived up to my imagination.

To the left was a bookstore, tall wooden shelves that reached almost to the ceiling, filled with an odd assortment of hardback, paper and leather bound books. Six rows of shelves, in fact, in two groupings of three, with a six-foot wide space between the two groups. There were three tables, each with three chairs, lined up in the space. At the far table, near a wall that was painted a sickly shade of gray and covered with strange symbols, a youngish looking man with long, unkempt hair that hung almost to his eyes, sat hunched over a large leather bound book, a large white mug at his elbow. Three large circular light fixtures hung from the ceiling, one over each table. There was a rectangular fluorescent light in each row between the shelves, casting just enough light to allow browsers to read the titles on the spines of the books. Three large glass cases sat along the wall near the bookshelves, containing jars, vials, boxes, and bottles. A small glass case with vents in the sides sat atop the middle case. Inside were three plants with oval green leaves and shaped purple and white flowers shaped like miniature champagne flutes.

The right side of the room was given over to the coffee shop. In the back was a counter, behind which stood two large cafeteria style coffee urns. Beside the urns were shelves containing large white coffee mugs, and containers of cream and sugar. To the right of the counter was a door. There was no sign, so I took this to be the access to the second floor. The space in front of the counter had six tables, each with three chairs, spaced about so that there was a semblance of privacy for customers, of which at the moment there were none.

Behind the counter stood a short woman with lank blonde hair that framed an oval face, and curtained down over her forehead. She was eying me curiously as I approached the counter, not smiling, not frowning; just watching. She held one of the large white mugs, cupping it against her breasts with both hands

"What'll it be?" she asked as I reached the counter.

"Are you Penelope Payton?" I asked.

"Yes, I am, why?"

Not a very voluble sort, I could see. She continued to regard me with that unreadable expression. I took out my ID and held it up so that she could see it.

"I was wondering if I might have a few moments of your time," I said.

"Are you a reporter?" she said, without looking at my ID. I held it closer to her face. She peered at it. "Why does a private investigator want to talk to me?"

"I'd like to talk to you about Henry Waylon."

The first flicker of emotion crossed her face. A muscle below her left eye twitched.

"What's there to talk about," she said quietly. "Henry's dead."

"I know that. I also know that he was innocent. Wouldn't you like to know what really happened? I know I would."

"I *know* what happened." Her light blue eyes blazed. "They killed an innocent man. They *knew* he was innocent, too, but they went ahead and did it anyway."

She was clutching the mug so tightly now, I was afraid she'd shatter it.

"Look, if you'd just give me a few minutes of your time," I said. "If you could just tell me what you know about what happened back then, it might . . . it would help with a case I'm working on."

Looking into her eyes, the way she seemed to stare right through me, I didn't think asking her directly if she'd threatened anyone would work. If I could get her talking, though, it might give me a sense of what she was capable of.

"I . . . okay, I guess I can spare a few minutes." She looked around. "Only have one customer, and he'll nurse that one coffee for the next two hours." When she looked back at me, she finally appeared to be looking *at* me. "Would you like a cup of coffee?"

I agreed, and she poured two mugs, handing me one. She then led me to the table in the front corner of the shop and sat with her back to the counter, but positioned so that she could see the entrance. Out from behind the counter, I could see that she was tall, almost as tall as me, and, while not beautiful in a traditional sense, had a pleasing face. I couldn't tell much about her figure. The light blue granny dress she wore covered her almost to her ankles. The way it draped over her figure, all I could see was that she had fairly generous breasts and broad shoulders. She wore what my grandmother would have called 'sensible' shoes; closed toes and flat heels, and her hips didn't sway or roll when she walked.

I sat in the chair to her left, with the big window to my left and solid wall behind me, where I could also watch the door. I took a sip of the coffee. I didn't recognize the flavor, but it wasn't bad. I sighed and took another sip.

"Good coffee," I said. "Where do you get it?"

She finally smiled at me over the lip of her mug. "I have a friend who has a friend," she said. "He gets the beans from a plantation in Togo, that's in West Africa. I grind the beans myself."

I held the cup up and sniffed. The coffee had a deep, woody aroma, stronger than Colombian, but not as harsh as the Arabica out of Vietnam.

"Think you could get your friend to sell me a few bags?"

She nodded. "Sure, leave me your contact information, and I'll let you know what he says. Now, you said you wanted to talk about . . . Henry's case."

It was either the coffee or my stunning personality, but she was suddenly becoming . . . voluble. She still had a sad look in her eyes.

I took my notebook out and opened it on the table. "You mind if I take notes?" She shook her head. "Okay, let's start with how long you knew Henry."

"We met during freshman orientation," she said. "It was just happenstance that we were seated next to each other. I dropped my pen, and Henry picked it up and handed it back to me. When our eyes met, I knew . . . just knew that he was the one."

"The one what?" I feigned ignorance, which caused her lips to twitch upwards ever so slightly.

"My soulmate, the man I wanted to spend the rest of my life with. I could tell the way he sort of stared back at me like a deer caught in headlights that he felt something too, but it took him a while to recognize what it was. When it did, though . . . well, we were practically inseparable after that. It helped that we were both pre-med."

I looked around. She didn't miss the look on my face.

"After Henry . . . well, afterwards, I just lost interest. Henry and I were planning to go to Africa or South America after we completed med school, and open a clinic to provide care to people who have no access to doctors. When they . . . when . . ."

"You dropped out of the pre-med program?" I finished for her.

"At first, yes," she said. "We were going into our senior year. I switched to Medieval History and Literature, but mid-way through my senior year, I just dropped out of school entirely. My family was well off, and when my parents died they left me a sizeable chunk of money. I used it to open this place. It was a way to . . . stay close to . . . well, you don't really want to hear all that."

Actually, I did want to hear all that, but I decided not to press her.

"So, what can you tell me about the night of the incident?"

"What's there to tell? Henry, Chuck and Mike were going out for drinks to celebrate the end of finals," she said. "I would have gone along, but a sorority sister in the house where I lived was having some serious problems, so I stayed in to take care of her. I didn't know about what happened until the next day when Chuck called and told me the police had taken Henry away."

"Chuck is Charles Armstrong, right?"

She nodded. "Yes, and Mike is Michael Fletcher. The three of them shared an apartment over on Twenty-First Street."

This was where it could get tricky. Since she wasn't a first-hand witness, asking her about the incidents in Virginia would do no good. What I needed to do was get her talking about how she felt about Waylon's trial and conviction.

"Did you attend the . . . trial?"

"Yes, I was there every day, right up until the end. I'd approached his attorney about testifying on his behalf, you know, a character witness, but he said it wouldn't do any good, so I was able to be in the courtroom."

"How well did you know Way-, Henry's sister?"

"Yolanda? Not well," she said. "I'd never met her before the trial. She was only a teenager, and after I did meet her, I got the sense she wasn't happy about her brother dating a white girl. She never said anything, but I got that feeling."

"Did you get along with his roommates?"

"Sure, we got along okay. I especially liked Chuck, and he simply adored Henry. Mike was okay, although he could be a bit of a cold fish sometimes."

"Explain."

"I don't know exactly, it was like he was always kind of looking down his nose at you or something. He was friendly enough I suppose, but somehow it never felt genuine."

Now was the time to edge her gently toward the subject that might give me a clue about her viability as the author of the threatening note.

"I suppose you were pretty upset," I said. "When the verdict was announced, and later when the judge passed sentence?"

"Yes, I was upset at the verdict," she said. There was a note of tired sadness in her voice. "But, I wasn't surprised. That jury was a bunch of old white people, and they didn't like Henry from the first day of the trial—I could tell from the way they looked at him and at their body language."

She held her cup up and blew into it. Then, she took a long sip.

"I guess I kinda lost it when the judge sentenced him to death," she went on after putting her cup back on the table. "I mean, he had the option of a life sentence. It just seemed so harsh. I think I might have screamed or cried out. But, Henry's sister, though, she went ballistic. They had to drag her out of the courtroom. I think if she could've gotten her hands on that judge, she would have scratched his eyes out . . . I know I felt like doing it."

"Have you had any contact with the

judge, or anyone else connected with the case since then?"

"Well, except for Henry's defense attorney, I didn't have any real contact with anyone even then. The detective from Arlington who was investigating came to talk to me, but when he learned that I wasn't around the night of the . . . incident, he ended the interview, and didn't talk to me anymore."

"How do you feel about them, especially the judge?"

Her eyes narrowed to two slits. Two spots of red appeared on her cheeks.

"How do I feel?" Her voice was tight. "I feel that they should all rot in hell, is how I feel. They killed an innocent man. Henry was one of the gentlest, kindest people I've ever known in my life."

"Would you ever act on that feeling?"

"You mean, would I do them harm?" She looked down at her coffee cup. "Would I want them to pay for what they did? If I had the opportunity . . . I think I'd happily kill them all."

EIGHTEEN

She hadn't actually confessed to threatening Carson, but the tone of her voice made it clear that he wouldn't shed any tears if he should come to harm. Of course, in her shoes, I'd probably have been feeling the same.

At any rate, there wasn't much more I could really ask her. Oh, I could have asked directly if she'd sent the judge a threatening note, but I doubt she would have admitted to it. Like, Yolanda Waylon, she didn't strike me as the type. Not that I was even sure what that was.

So, I finished my coffee, gave her one of my cards, and left her sitting there, alone in her shop with one customer still hunched over his book, and went back to my car.

I drove from her shop to the clinic, hoping Michael Fletcher would be working.

I was in luck. He was, and the same receptionist from my first visit had me wait for him. The waiting room was more crowded than before, with four rows of chairs filled. I noticed that the ratio of Hispanic to black patients was about one to one, and the coughing and hacking was greater than it had been before, so I took a chair in the very last row, this time closer to the exit than the wall.

I'd only been waiting a few minutes when the door in the mural opened. A tall man, almost my height, wearing neat, dark green scrubs walked into reception from the back. He had a square jaw, with sandy blond, close-cropped hair, and green eyes set close together. He looked over toward me and started walking my way, ignoring the patients who tried to get his attention as he passed them.

He entered the empty row of chairs in front of me, walked over to the end and sat in the one in front of me. He turned and draped his right arm over the back of the chair. His thin lips were set in a straight line, and his gaze was at a point just below my chin.

"You must be Pennyback, the private eye," he said. "Chuck said you might be coming by to talk to me."

Didn't seem to make much sense showing him my ID, but I did it anyway. It's a habit. Besides, it saves grief later if some asshole decides he didn't like the questions I was asking—at least, he can't claim I didn't let him know up front who I was.

"If you don't mind, I'd like to ask you a few questions about the Henry Waylon case."

"Shoot," he said.

"Is there somewhere we could talk with a bit more privacy?"

Already, heads on the row just ahead of us were beginning to turn our way.

"Well, there's a sandwich shop just down the street. It's usually not crowded this time of day," he said. "I'd use one of the examining rooms like Chuck did, but all our doctors are here today, and they're pretty busy back there." He looked around at the reception room, an expression of distaste on his face.

Some bedside manner, I thought, wondering why someone with his attitude would bother working in a free clinic. He stood and moved toward the exit. I rose and followed.

Sandwiches, Subs, and Soups was in the middle of the next block. Except for an elderly brown skin woman with the sunken jaw of someone with no teeth, the place was empty.

"Somethin' I can get y'all?" she said as we entered. The sight of her slightly blue gums validated my guess that she was toothless, and robbed me of any appetite I might have had.

"Just coffee, black," I said.

"Same for me," Fletcher added.

"Jest set anywhere you want," the toothless hag said. "I'll bring yo coffee right out."

` The place was small, slightly smaller than the clinic's reception area, with twelve tables in two rows of six, in front of the counter. We sat in the table just inside the entrance to the right. I took the farthest chair, giving me a view of the street through the large plate glass window, and the left half of the interior. I wasn't comfortable having two tables at my back, but with no other customers, I figured I could put up with it for the short time I'd planned to use to ask Fletcher a few questions.

The old lady brought two Styrofoam cups containing a dark, almost black, liquid.

Steam billowed up from the surface.

"How much?" I asked.

"Six dollah," she said. A line of brownish liquid hung from the left side of her mouth.

It was highway robbery, but I could put it on my expense report. Isaac Carson could afford it.

"I'd like a receipt please."

The old woman gave me an evil look, and made a snorting sound, as I held up a ten spot. She snatched the note and whirled around. Her shoes, which I couldn't see beneath the floor length dress draping her bony hips, made a clumping sound on the uneven wood floor. She came back shortly with a slip of cash register tape, which she dropped on the table next to my coffee.

Fletcher stared down at his coffee.

"You don't really plan on drinking this shit, do you?" he asked.

"Not in this life," I said. "But, we couldn't just use the lady's tables for free."

He laughed and eased his cup to one side.

"Okay, what do you want to know?"

"Why don't you walk me through what happened that night in Arlington," I said. "Where you went, who you met, what you did?"

"I don't know if there's anything I can tell you that you haven't already heard from Chuck."

"I'd like to hear your version of the evening, though," I said.

"Well, okay. We'd decided to go out and have some fun," he said. "We'd just finished our final exams, and Chuck figured we owed ourselves a celebration." He put a finger to the tip of his nose and half closed his eyes. "We started out in Georgetown. Hit a few bars along M Street. Then, we decided to walk over to Rosslyn and try some of the places over there. I remember we were already pretty buzzed by then."

As he talked, he looked steadily down at the coffee cup. His brows wrinkled as if he was deep in concentration.

"Do you remember where you went?"

"I don't recall the name, just that it was up Wilson Avenue a ways. We walked over from Georgetown. It was a bit of a dive, though, all dim lights, loud music, and even louder talk. I think it must have been a front for hookers. There were a lot of overly made and under-dressed women there. Anyway, we weren't there more than a few minutes when this blonde bimbo attached herself to Henry like a remora to a shark."

"This *bimbo* wouldn't happen to be the girl who was later found raped and murdered, would it?"

He at least had the decency to look embarrassed. His cheeks darkened, but he still wouldn't look me in the eye.

"Uh, yeah, it was," he said. "I guess that did come off sounding a little uncaring." He didn't sound like he really cared that it'd sounded uncaring. "That's her, though. She kept rubbing herself up against Henry. Hell, if he hadn't been son dark, his blushing would've lit that joint up."

"Was he responding to her advances at all?"

"He was a dude, wasn't he? The chick was rubbing her tits against his arms and her crotch against his leg. Damn right he reacted."

"So," I asked. "What happened next?"

He looked down at his cup, and then off to his right. Just a flicker of his eyes, but to me a sure sign that he was about to lie.

"Well, we'd been in the place about . . . oh, half an hour, or a bit more," he said. "Henry said he was feeling woozy, probably from all the booze he'd had. Said he was going outside for some fresh air. I don't remember too much after that. I was pretty bombed myself by that time."

"Did he come back inside?"

"I honestly don't remember. I don't think so."

"What about the girl? What did she do?"

He did the eye flickering again. "I don't recall. She just wasn't there after a while. I don't remember seeing her leave."

I was mentally processing his story. In general, it seemed to agree with what Armstrong had told me, differing in some of the details. Some of the differences were understandable. I would have been suspicious if they'd agreed in every detail. But, a couple of the differences were significant. I filed them away for further thought.

"How did you get along with Waylon?" I asked.

He looked into my eyes for the first time. Just briefly, before his gaze flickered off to the left.

"How'd I get along with him? Fine. We were classmates and roommates."

"I've only seen the pictures of him taken when he was arrested," I said. "But, he looked a pretty good looking guy. I imagine that he was pretty popular with the ladies."

"Yeah, the chicks on campus liked old Henry." There was tightness in his voice. Barely noticeable. Most people wouldn't even have caught it, but I've had a lot of experience with people who are trying to hide things. I caught it, but I kept my expression neutral, hoping he wouldn't notice, which was hardly necessary, since he still refused to look directly at me. "He had a girlfriend, though—Penny Payton. She was a pre-med student, too. I think they'd been hooking up since freshman year. So, on campus, old Henry was pretty circumspect."

"Are you saying he had other women, just off campus?"

"Well, I can't say for sure, but if I was a betting man, I'd say, yeah. I mean, what guy's gonna turn free ass down?"

I sat there for a few seconds looking at him, willing him to look me in the eye. He didn't take the bait. I couldn't think of anything else to ask him. I needed to dig deeper to see what was going on here. Fletcher had a thing about Waylon, but I couldn't pin it down—just a nagging feeling I had in the back of my brain.

"Okay," I said. "Thanks for your time. If I think of any more questions, is it okay if I drop by?"

"Sure, I'm at the clinic almost every day except Saturday and Sunday."

I put a dollar tip on the table and left, my coffee cold and untouched. The old woman flashed me a toothless smile as I walked out. As I walked back toward my car, I glanced over my shoulder. Fletcher was standing outside the coffee shop looking at me.

NINETEEN

I'd just fastened my seat belt and was about to insert the key in the ignition when my phone rang. I unfastened the belt, pulled the phone from my pants and answered. It was Heather.

"Al," she said. "I just got a call from Malcolm Jenkins. He's agreed to speak with you."

"When and where?"

"As soon as you can get there. He's in private practice now. Has an office on Rockville Pike, near White Flint Mall."

She gave me the address and rang off.

It took me twenty minutes to navigate the traffic across town to Wisconsin Avenue, and another twenty north on Wisconsin to get to the area near White Flint Mall, a big shopping plaza on the east side of Rockville Pike. Jenkins's office was on the second floor of a small strip mall on the west side of the pike, three blocks north of White Flint. The ground floor business were mainly small independent operations, including a jewelry shop and a toy store, while the upper level seemed to be mostly professionals who couldn't afford the rent in the larger office complexes. The little parking area in front of place was crowded, but I managed to squeeze the Bug into a slot near the south end. I had to walk back to the center to take the stairs up to the second level and then all the way to the north end to get to his office.

The receptionist, a small Asian girl with the wide flat cheekbones of a Korean sat in a tiny outer office which was just large enough for her desk and a small three cushion sofa with a glass top coffee table in front of it. When I showed her my ID, she just nodded and told me to go right in, that 'Mr. Carsuwell' was waiting for me.

Jenkins's private office was somewhat larger, with a large executive desk facing the door, a floor to ceiling book case full of thick legal looking books to the left, and a larger sofa and two chairs with a clone of the glass top coffee table to the right.

He stood as I entered. My height, and probably a pound or two heavier, but flab instead of muscle, Jenkins was younger looking than I'd expected. Even with the thinning brown hair swept back on his round head, and the rimless glasses that magnified his dark brown eyes, he didn't look more than forty-five.

"Mr. Pennyback," he said, coming from behind the desk with his pudgy hand extended. "You made good time. Your associate said you were over in Northeast.

The traffic can't have been pleasant."

His grip was soft, and his hands were slick with perspiration, but his gaze was level, and his voice was clear and strong.

"Yeah, it was a bit rough, especially between Connecticut and Wisconsin."

I released his hand as quickly as I could without giving offense. I hate wet handshakes. He motioned me to the sofa, and took the chair to my left.

"Well now, you want to talk about the Henry Waylon case? What would you like to know?"

His expression was sad.

"Anything you can tell me," I said. I didn't want to tell him any details of my investigation—not just yet. "That must have been one of your early cases, right?"

"Ah, yes—say, would you like some refreshment . . . coffee or tea perhaps?"

I like coffee, maybe a bit too much, but I'd had two cups with breakfast and the large mug with Penelope Payton. Besides, the picture of that noxious liquid served by the toothless old woman was still in my mind.

"Tea would be fine," I said.

"Excellent choice." He stood and opened the door. "Miss Han, could we get a pot of that excellent jasmine tea of yours?"

Her mumbled response was cut off as he shut the door.

"You'll like Miss Han's jasmine tea," he said after he'd sat back down. "It's really refreshing. Much better for you than coffee in fact."

I leaned forward, frowning at him, and made a production of removing my notebook and pen from my pocket.

"Ah yes," he said. "You think perhaps I'm using delaying tactics? Well, I suppose you're right. No; in fact, you're absolutely right. Henry Waylon's case was not my finest hour as a lawyer. I keep thinking that if I'd been a better lawyer he would never have been convicted, or if I'd worked harder, I would have won an appeal."

"There's no point beating yourself up, Mr. Jenkins," I said. "I imagine you did the best you could."

There was a light rapping on the door, and the receptionist came in with a small square plastic tray upon which was a small ceramic teapot and two cups. She put the tray on the table and silently withdrew. There were small packets of sugar next to the pot.

Jenkins busied himself filling the two cups with an amber liquid. He pushed one toward me and picked up the other.

"Would you care for sugar with yours?"

"No thank you," I said.

"Good idea. This jasmine tea is imported from Korea by Miss Han's father. She gets it for me at a big discount. It's really much better without sugar." He blew on it and took a sip.

I followed his lead. It was good. There was just the slightest hint of jasmine in the aroma and flavor. I put my cup down and took up my notebook again.

"Quite right," he said. "No more dilly dallying. Where to start? I suppose I might as well start at the beginning, right? After passing the bar, I took a job as a public defender. My law school grades weren't good enough to interest any of the big firms, and I thought it would be a good way to get some courtroom experience."

He took another sip of tea. A wistful experience crossed his face.

"I'd done a couple of cases before Henry's," he continued. "Mostly Latino immigrants who'd violated some arcane public ordinance with which they were unfamiliar. The population of Spanish speakers was starting to really increase around that time. Anyway, when Henry's case came in, for some reason, none of the other lawyers in the office wanted to touch it, so when the director asked me, I jumped at the chance. I mean, a rape and murder trial . . . I figured it would provide me a lot of experience."

"Was that normal . . . assigning such an inexperienced lawyer to such a serious case?"

"Well, yes and no," he said. "The way it worked was, the most senior guys got to sort of pick the cases they worked, and the rest of us were assigned what was left. When they found out that the ADA prosecuting Henry would be Tom Macauley, the senior guys didn't want to have anything to do with it. I was the most junior lawyer in the system at the time, so the supervisor just dumped it into my lap."

More and more, Macauley, the prosecutor who had allegedly withheld evidence favorable to the defendant, was figuring in this case. He was someone I definitely wanted a shot at.

"What was so special about Macauley?" I asked.

"Well, I didn't find out until the trial was well underway . . . actually, not until it was almost over, but Macauley had a reputation as a hardline prosecutor, one who would do almost anything to win."

"Anything, including maybe withholding evidence that he should have shared with the defense?"

His eyes went round and his hand stopped with his tea cup halfway to his mouth.

"That wouldn't just be unethical," he said. He shook his head. "That would very well be a crime. I have a hard time believing even Macauley would . . . wait, are you referring to the DNA evidence? Do you think he knew about that during the trial?"

"I can't prove it, but that's the rumor I've heard, and from a pretty reliable source."

Actually, I'd heard it third-hand, but Lucy's reliable, and she felt her source was reliable, and from what I was hearing about this guy, Macauley, it was beginning to sound credible.

He put his cup down so hard, even though it was only half full, tea sloshed over the rim. It was a wonder, in fact, that the fragile looking cup didn't shatter.

"That son of a bitch," he said. "I knew he was a snake, but that's way over the line."

"Not much to be done about it now, I suppose."

"The hell there isn't. If that allegation could be proven, he'd be disbarred at a minimum, and possibly even prosecuted." Then his face fell. "Of course, after all this time, proving it's going to be difficult."

It wouldn't be much, but it would be a small measure of justice for Waylon I thought. I leaned forward.

"Look, I'm gonna share something with

you," I said. "But, you need to keep it in strictest confidence. Can you do that?"

"If it's legal, I suppose I could. But, I'll have no part in anything illegal."

"There's nothing illegal. I have a client who feels he's being threatened because of his involvement in Henry Waylon's conviction, and I'm trying to identify the person doing the threatening. With the reports that the DNA evidence exonerates the kid, I'm also determined to find out who actually *did* do it."

"Good luck with that," he said. "If the cops haven't found anything after ten years, what makes you think you can?"

I laughed. "For starters, it it's true that evidence *was* withheld, the cops aren't gonna be all that anxious to find the real killer, now are they?" He frowned and nodded. "So, here's my deal for you—if I can find proof that this Macauley character did deliberately withhold evidence, will you follow it up and take action against him?"

For the first time since I'd entered his office he smiled.

"With pleasure," he said.

TWENTY

By Tuesday morning I'd given up on trying to beat Heather to the office. I know a fluke when it slaps me on the nose. I got to work at 8:15, and as expected, she was already there and was busy at her computer. She looked up and smiled when I walked in.

"Hey, boss, what's on for today?"

"Do you have an address for Thomas Macauley?" I asked.

"Sure, but why? He hasn't returned my call requesting an appointment yet."

And, I didn't expect him to. The guy was probably cowering in his office hoping I'd lose interest and go away. Well, I had no intention of going away.

"I don't think he's gonna call, so if the mountain won't come to Mohammed . . . well, you know the rest."

"How is talking to Macauley helping find out who it is that's threatening our client?"

"Oh, that," I said. "My money's on either Yolanda Waylon or Penelope Payton for that . . . although I can't prove it . . . but, I can't see either of them as actually following up on the threats."

She gave me her most serious schoolmarm look. "That's it? You're going to tell Carson that he's being threatened by one of two women, but not to worry?"

"Well, of course not. I'm still working on it. But, this Waylon case is starting to get under my skin. I have to find out a few things more and I might . . ."

"Never mind," she said. "I might have known you were off on another of your damned quests. Okay, if you're gonna beard the lion in his den you'd better be about it."

TWENTY-ONE

Thomas Macauley no longer worked for the district attorney's office. Like Jenkins, he'd foregone government work for private practice. But, unlike Jenkins, who worked alone, Macauley had become senior partner in the firm of Johnson, Ellicott, and Macauley, a law firm that specialized in representing large defense contractors. Their office was a modernistic structure on Ninth and Kent Streets in Pentagon City, a trendy shopping district south of the Pentagon across I-395.

The single story building was mostly glass and steel, with a brown and ochre brick hip wall, well landscaped gardens on the sides, and a futuristic fountain in front. Parking was behind the building, reached by a privet hedge-lined driveway off Ninth Street. I pulled around and found myself in a huge parking lot containing ten or fifteen expensive Mercedes, Beamers, and other cars, each of which cost more than I made in a year. Among the overpriced wheels were a few Toyotas and Hondas, probably owned by secretaries and associates. I pulled into an empty space between a BMW and a Honda Civic, and walked back around to the front.

The reception area was a low-ceiling room that took up a goodly portion of the front of the building, with a large, black desk on the right that looked like the flight control deck of a space ship, behind which sat a regal looking blonde wearing a blue and white designer suit complete with white silk scarf and a snotty expression on her well-made-up face. On the left, arranged in tasteful little groups were low back, black leather chairs grouped in twos around round black metal tables. Slim urns were interspersed here and there containing ferns and other indoor plants. Behind all this were three hallways, spaced equidistance along the walls, down which I could see doors on each side. It was hard to tell, but it looked like four or five doors on each side of each hallway. Including space for a law library and conference room, there had to be at least thirty employees.

The receptionist eyed me as I approached. The way her icy blue eyes narrowed, I felt like looking down to make sure my fly was closed.

"May I help you?" Her voice was as icy as her gaze.

"I'd like to see Thomas Macauley," I said.

She typed on her keyboard and then looked at a large monitor. "I'm sorry, what is your name?"

"Pennyback, Al Pennyback."

"I'm really sorry Mr. . . . Pennyback, but you're not on Mr. Macauley's schedule for today.

Blondie with the icy voice and dead blue

eyes was beginning to get under my skin.

"I'm not on the schedule," I said. "Because your boss, or maybe you, haven't responded to my request for an appointment."

She took a step backwards, and brought a hand to her breasts, just below the point of her scarf.

"Really, sir, there's no need to raise your voice," she said.

I looked around. Several doors in all three of the hallways were opened, and people were gathering at the entrance to the hallways.

"Oh, I don't know. Seems like a raised voice is what it takes to get attention around here. I want to speak to Thomas Macauley."

"Sir, really," she said. "If you don't leave, I'll be forced to call the police."

I moved around until I had her between me and the back wall, holding my hands up in a non-threatening manner.

"Okay, hold on, there's no need for that," I said. "I just want to talk to Thomas Clayton. It's very important. Could you at least call him and ask him if he'd see me?"

Human nature is quirky. When people sense a conflict, rather than ignoring it, or even better, moving the hell away, they move toward it like moths to a light bulb. Like the rubberneckers who slow down on the highway when they see a car crash. The denizens of the offices in the back of Johnson, Ellicott, and Macauley were no different. Someone in one of the near offices had no doubt heard my raised voice, and had stuck his or her head out to see what was going on. Seeing the altercation, that person had probably told someone else, and the office grapevine had done the work.

Dozens of pairs of eyes were glued to the tableau in front of the reception desk—one of their own was being intimidated by this hulking black man. Typical of people, though; no one made a move to do anything about it.

I scanned the three groups of watchers, and there, in the group clustered at the entrance to the center hallway, I spotted my target.

He was of medium height, probably five-ten or eleven, and looked to be in his late forties, but tan and fit. His gray suit was impeccably tailored and hung on him well, and his sandy hair was neatly trimmed and combed straight back on his oval head. What marked him, though, was that, while everyone else stared inquisitively, with expressions of mild confusion, his face bore a look of near panic.

I stepped to the side and pointed directly at him. He shrank back behind two young women.

"Macauley," I said. "Why won't you respond to my partner's phone calls? I need to talk to you about the Waylon case."

He looked to right and left with jerky motions, and then back in my direction. There was fear in his grey eyes.

"I have nothing to say to you," he said in a weak voice. "Now, unless you leave, I'll have Janice call the police and have you forcibly removed."

I didn't want to push it that far, and I did want to talk to him. For now, though, I'd be satisfied with just stirring things up a little.

"We do have things to talk about, you and I—things like withholding of evidence. I'm leaving now, Macauley, but you haven't seen the last of me."

I couldn't have known that he *had*, in fact, seen the last of me.

TWENTY-TWO

The next day, I was sitting at my desk with Heather's list of names and my list of things I'd learned spread out before me, my head cupped in my hands, at a complete loss as to how to move my case forward.

Heather pushed my door open and came halfway in.

"Al, Buster's here with a cop from . . ."

Buster pushed gently past her before she could finish. Following in his wake was a small framed white guy wearing an ill-fitting brown suit; his black buzz cut hair sprinkled with grey.

"Hey, bro," Buster said in his booming voice. "Hate to barge in, but we got to talk."

Buster's always welcome, but I sensed from the look on his face that this wasn't a social visit, and that the subject would be unpleasant.

"Make yourselves at home," I said. I pointed to the single chair beside my desk. "Heather, could you please roll another chair in for our visitors?"

She ducked back into her office, returning a few moments later, pushing her wheeled visitor's chair, which she placed on the right side of my desk. Buster took that chair, leaving his friend to take the chair to my left.

"Al," Buster said. "This is Detective Sergeant Peter Simpson from the Arlington County Police Department."

Simpson extended a hand. I shook it. His handshake was firm, and his hand was dry.

"Pleased to meet you, Mr. Pennyback, I've heard a lot about you."

"Thanks," I said. I looked at Buster. "To what do I owe the pleasure of this visit?"

Buster nodded at Simpson.

"Mr. Pennyback, I understand you paid a visit to the offices of one Thomas Macauley yesterday?"

He phrased it as a question, but from his expression, I knew that he already knew the answer.

"Yes, I did."

"And, is it true that you threatened him?"

I glared at him, and then shot a quizzical look at Buster, who merely shrugged.

"No, I didn't really *threaten* him." I guess technically what I said to him could be considered a threat of sorts. "Look, I'm working on a case, and he has information that might be important to it. He's refused to talk to me, so I went by his office to rattle his cage. I guess if he called in a complaint, it must have worked."

Simpson looked from me to Buster.

"Told you it'd be a waste of time," Buster said.

Now, I was confused. The two of them seemed to know something I didn't.

"Would someone tell me what's going on here?" I asked.

"Macauley didn't file a complaint against you," Simpson said. "I'm just closing up loose ends. Thomas Macauley was found dead this morning around 6:45 in a small park near his condo in Arlington."

"Whoa! You're not saying you think I killed him?"

Simpson's expression shut down. He got that stone-faced look that cops get when they know something but they don't want you to know they know it.

"No, I don't think you killed him," he said. "In fact, I can't be sure . . . Detective Mayweather here vouches for you, and that's good enough for me. I was just wondering . . . what case are you working on?"

Ah ha, I thought. That's it. The cops are wondering if Macauley's death is connected to my investigation. Hell, I'm starting to wonder myself. But, two can play at the game of 'I Know Something You Don't Know.'

"I'm sorry, Detective Simpson," I said in my most innocent sounding voice. "I'm not at liberty to discuss my case. The privacy of my client, you know." Then, I realized something. He'd never said how Macauley died. "What was the cause of death, by the way?"

"I'm not really at liberty to say," Simpson said, giving me a taste of my own medicine.

Buster made a growling noise deep in his throat.

"Come on, Pete," he said. "It'll probably be all over the fucking papers by the evening edition. Might's well tell him."

Simpson didn't look too happy, but he cleared his throat. "Well, right now, we don't know for sure," he said. "But, it looked like a heart attack."

"Since when do the police investigate heart attacks?"

"Since a man who just passed his physical with flying colors, and who runs in two marathons a year has one," he said.

"I take it, then, that you don't think it was actually a heart attack."

He smiled, showing his teeth. The guy might be a lousy dresser, but he showed the feral instincts of a pit bull. He was someone I'd hate to have after me.

"Until I see an autopsy report," he said. "I'm not ready to accept death by natural causes."

TWENTY-THREE

Simpson thanked me for my time, and left me one of his name cards with the request that if I thought of anything to give him a call. Buster said he'd be calling me later, and the two of them left.

They left me with one more piece of a puzzle that had no picture as a guide, and no pieces that seemed to fit with any other pieces. Thomas Macauley was now no longer in the picture. Like Detective Simpson, I wasn't ready to accept death by natural causes. That would be entirely too coincidental, and despite what I'd said to Heather, I don't believe in that kind of coincidence.

I was still convinced that the truth behind the Waylon case was somehow at the bottom of this whole mess. Macauley's death, however, removed one of the people who could provide clarity to things, leaving just two; Allan Bavan, a possibly dirty cop who had conspired to send an innocent man to his death, and the person who had actually committed the crime for which Henry Waylon was executed.

It was time to turn the screws on Bavan just a little tighter.

I let Heather know where I was going and walked down to Water Street.

Bavan wasn't sitting on his back deck. In fact, the houseboat looked deserted.

I stopped at the foot of the gangplank, looking for any sign that he was aboard. I'm not fond of boats, ships, or anything else that doesn't traverse dry land, and most of all, I've never understood all the protocol and rigmarole associated with going onboard one of the damned things. But, the boat owners I know, Quincy Chang being one of them, are pretty stuffy about it.

"Hello . . . ahoy, Allan Bavan," I called. "Request permission to come aboard."

I was about to say the hell with it and step aboard, when a Colt 9mm barrel, followed by the grip held in a beefy hand, emerged from the dark opening beyond the rear deck. "Stop right where you are," Bavan's alcohol blurred voice said. "Until I can get a better look at you."

He was a shadowy figure in the gloomy light, leaning in from the right side of the door. After thirty of the longest seconds I can remember since waiting for the green light on the door frame of a C-130 so I could hurl my body into the darkness of night from an altitude of 5,000 feet, he himself entered the door frame, giving me a clear view.

"Sorry, Pennyback," he said, lowering the weapon, but still glancing right and left. "Can't be too careful, and my eyes ain't what they used to be. Come on aboard."

I boarded, and he motioned me to join him inside the cabin, which was furnished in what I assumed was a sailor's version of a living room. A wood frame sofa that looked like it converted into a bed, with a rectangular table bolted to the floor . . . deck . . . in front. Waist-high cabinets lined the right and left walls, or as the sailors called them, starboard and port bulkheads. I had trouble remembering which was right and which was left. There was a half-empty bottle of Jack Daniels and an empty water glass on the table.

"What's with the gun?" I asked.

He put it down on the table next to the JD and flopped back onto the sofa. He motioned me to a deck chair in the corner.

"Have a sit down," he said. "Sorry 'bout waving a piece in your face like that, but your last visit spooked me, I guess."

"Has anyone threatened you?"

He picked up the bottle and filled the glass almost to the brim. Then, still holding the bottle in his right hand, he lifted the glass with his left and drained off half its contents. After putting both back on the table, he wiped his mouth with his forearm and looked at me, blinking as if he was having trouble focusing.

"I guesh, er, guess, I was a little spooked after your visit," he said. "You refused to tell me, but I figure it must've been that ADA, Macauley, who's getting threats, and if somebody's after him, I'm likely to be next on the list."

Even from five feet away and with no air moving in the small room, the smell of stale booze and sour breath coming from was enough to make my eyes sting. I tried taking shallow breaths to minimize the impact, not that it really helped. He was wearing an off-purple Redskins tee-shirt that was stained dark under his arms and smeared with crusted stains across the bulge of his belly. When he moved his arms, the musty smell of his underarms joined with the booze and breath, making me wish I was somewhere far away and upwind of him.

"Why would anyone want to threaten you?" I asked.

He took another drink and looked at me with bloodshot eyes.

"Hey, I don't have a radio or TV here, but after you left, I went out and dug up some old copies of the *Post*. I saw the stories about the DNA, and some reporter's sayin' the state done that kid Waylon wrong. I was the lead investigator, so some of the shit's bound to splash on me."

He spoke slowly, slurring some of his words. The more than half-empty bottle in front of him wasn't likely his first of the day. Then, he squinted at me and clamped his mouth shut. I had to handle him carefully. Even drunk, his cop instincts were probably still good.

"Yeah, but you were just doing your job," I said. "Why would anyone want to threaten you for that? For that matter, why do you think the prosecutor would be threatened?"

"Well, 'cause . . ." He snapped his lips shut, and glared at me. Finally, he shook his head. "You know how it is. These people always blame the cops and they system for anything bad that happens. The civil rights assholes will be out in force, yellin' police brutality, and shit like that."

"I don't recall there being any allegations of brutality in the Waylon case."

"Fuckin' A there wasn't," he said. "That case was done by the book . . . kid's rights were read to him, and nobody, and I mean nobody, put a hand on him."

"And, he was convicted by a jury and sentenced by a judge," I said. "But, now the evidence indicates that he was, in fact, innocent."

"What fuckin' evidence?" Spittle dribbled from the corners of his mouth and wound snakelike through the stubble on his chin.

"DNA evidence that was taken from the scene."

His eyes blinked slowly like someone just waking up.

"W-where'd you hear that?"

"From a reliable source," I said. "And, furthermore, I heard that the ADA knew about the evidence before the trial and withheld it from the defense."

He shook his head slowly from side to side.

"N-no, that can't be right. He wouldn't d-do that."

"Who wouldn't do what?"

He pushed himself up slowly, swaying, and had to balance himself on the arm of the sofa to keep from falling.

"N-nothing, never mind," he said. "I ain't got nothin' else to say to you. Get out."

"Look, if you're in trouble, maybe I can help."

"I said, get the fuck out!"

His face was ashen and tears streamed from his bloodshot eyes as he stood there swaying from side to side glaring at me.

Sometimes, the best thing to do is withdraw and come back at it another time. I stood and slowly backed from the room. When I hit the gangplank, I turned, but kept looking over my shoulder as I walked quickly away.

He never came out of the room.

TWENTY-FOUR

Sandra and I finished supper at 6:30 and were sitting on the back porch, watching a family of squirrels play tag with a herd of five deer at the edge of the forest, when I heard the rumble of a car at the front of the house.

"Are you expecting company?" Sandra asked.

"No," I said, rising from the rattan chair. "Probably someone looking for an address in the area. I'll go see who it is."

As I stepped off the porch, Buster came around the corner of the house.

"Hey, bro," he said. "Hope you don't mind me droppin' in without callin' first. Hey, Sandra, how're things going?"

Sandra came off the porch and embraced him, kissing him lightly on the cheek. "No problem, Buster," she said. "You know we're always happy to have you visit. How are Alma and the kids?"

"Doin' fine. They really liked havin' you guys over for the barbecue. We got to do that again soon." He turned to me. "I came out, 'cause I got some information back about the Macauley case, and I wanted to share it with you."

"Sure," I said. "Would you like a beer?"

"Is the Pope Catholic? Damn right I'd like a beer."

He bound up the steps, and grabbed a chair from the corner where I keep them stacked.

I started for the back door, but Sandra laid a hand on my arm. "That's okay, babe," she said. "I'll get it. You two have business to discuss."

I watched her backside as she entered the kitchen. More fun than watching squirrels and deer, for sure. When the door clicked shut behind her, I sat in the chair next to Buster.

"So, amigo," I said. "To what do I owe the pleasure of this visit?"

"The post-mortem just came back on Macauley. He died of a heart attack, but the ME found high levels of digitalis in his system."

"Digitalis . . . isn't that a medication used to treat heart disease?"

"Yeah, but according to the ME in a person with no heart condition, or if the dose is too high, it can actually cause cardiac arrest," he said. "And, in Thomas Macauley's case, he didn't have a condition, and there was a lot of that shit in his system."

That was interesting. Troubling, but interesting. Why would anyone use something like that to kill? How would someone use it?

"I don't know how much is a lot," I said. "But, how in hell do you poison someone with it?"

"They said he only had water, and some

kind of herbal tea and honey in his stomach, and nothing else, so the digitalis must have been in the tea. Problem is, the only thing found with the body was his water bottle, and it was clean. The cops searched his condo and found no signs of tea or honey, so they're pretty sure somebody slipped it to him somehow. "

"Hell, wouldn't he taste this digitalis?"

"I don't know," he said. "Maybe the honey masked the taste. I don't even know if this digitalis shit even has a taste."

"One thing's for sure, it's not something you can just buy at the drugstore, so either he did it to himself or someone did it for him."

Sandra came out with two large glasses of beer and a glass of white wine on a tray. She handed a beer to each of us, and took the wine for herself. After seating herself next to me, she took a sip.

"So, guys, what did I miss?"

Buster repeated what he'd told me.

"It was clearly murder," she said when he'd finished.

"What makes you say that?" he asked.

"The guy was a wealthy, successful lawyer," she said. "He had no reason to kill himself."

I looked at Buster. He nodded.

"She's right, bro. And, that's kinda what the cops over 'cross the river think. Problem is, they also don't have a motive for anybody to off the guy, 'leastways, not *that* way."

I could see his point. There'd probably be no shortage of ex-cons who had it in for a former ADA, but that kind of perp wouldn't go for something as exotic as poison. They'd just stick a shiv in him, shoot him, or if they were really pissed, bomb his car. Poison is the weapon of choice of a more sophisticated killer, or a woman, which brought my thinking back to my two main suspects in the Waylon case. The problem with either, though, is that in order to poison someone, you have to have access to the victim, and I couldn't see how either Yolanda Waylon or Penelope Payton could have gotten to Macauley, or how they might have gotten their hands on digitalis.

"So, they're treating it as a homicide? But, they have no suspects?"

"Well, they're treating it as a suspicious death for now—a possible homicide—and even though they don't think it was anyone he put away, they're checking every case he ever worked."

That, I knew, might eventually lead them to either of the two women. I decided to change the subject.

"You know the rumor that Macauley suppressed important evidence in the Waylon case," I said.

"Yeah, it's already going around," Buster said. "There's rumors he might have played fast and loose with the rules in a few other cases as well. They're trying to keep a lid on it, though, 'cause it might involve a few cops as well."

"So, the boys in blue are planning to close ranks to protect each other," Sandra said.

A muscle in Buster's jaw twitched. Sandra saw it, but she just smiled innocently at him.

"Okay, okay," he said. His massive

shoulders slumped. "I hate to admit it, but sometimes it happens. Internal Affairs tries to root out dirty cops, but sometimes you even get some rotten apples in IA."

Sandra still had an innocent look on her face, but as many of her students had learned over the years, it didn't mean she wasn't about to skewer them.

"But, in the Waylon case, those rotten apples caused the death of an innocent man," she said.

"Yeah, I know, you're probably right. But, most cops, the vast majority, are honest and play strictly by the rules. We go out there every day and put our lives on the line to protect people, and for what? You know the average salary for a cop in this country is about fifty-nine grand a year? You know how hard it is to live in most cities on that, especially if you have kids. And, don't even get me started on how people view cops. Hell, the only occupations that have a lower approval rating than cops is politicians and public schools. Hell, almost half the people in this country disapprove of us, and in minority communities, over half usually don't like or trust cops."

Sandra got up and walked over and laid a hand on his shoulder.

"I know, Buster," she said. "I know that it's unfair for people to feel the way they do about the police because of a few bad apples, but consider why those people feel the way they do."

"I can dig it. Don't forget, I come from one of those communities. I know what it's like to have a cop look at your black face and assume you're up to no good, despite the fact that 70-80 percent of the people in the 'hood are decent law abiding citizens. Problem is, when you're patrolling the streets, it's that 20 to 30 percent you have to look out for."

She put her arms around him and cradled his head against her shoulder.

"It's a problem that both sides need to work on," I said. "But, in the meantime, let's finish these beers before they get warm."

TWENTY-FIVE

The next morning, Heather delivered another piece of disturbing news.

"I did some digging into the backgrounds of everyone on our list," she said. "I found something interesting . . . and disturbing about Yolanda Waylon."

"Let me guess. In the army she wasn't really trained as a lab technician, but is in reality a trained assassin, and she's now working secretly for the CIA."

I laughed. She didn't.

"That's not even funny. Could you be serious just for a minute? You know I can't hack . . . er, get into the agency's computers."

She was totally serious. For Heather to admit that there was a computer system beyond her reach was . . . well, unprecedented.

"Okay, I'm sorry," I said. "What did you find out?"

"Yolanda's assigned to a lab at MedGen that is assessing the various medications used to treat heart disease."

I knew what was coming next, and I was sure I wasn't going to like what I heard.

"One of the medications they're testing is digitalis," she said.

I knew I wouldn't like it.

TWENTY-SIX

I was at that point in the case where more than meditation was needed. I needed some good, sound advice.

My source of advice, when all else failed, lived in a high-tech protected log cabin at the end of a twisty dirt road off River Road, a few miles beyond my farm house.

Carlton Raine, known not so affectionately by the nickname Blood by his former colleagues, was hired by the CIA in the 50s, becoming one of their first full-fledged black field agents. Oh, they had one or two in stations in Africa, but Blood was so adept at 'wet work,' what was euphemistically called 'direction action' in the agency, that he quickly became their go-to guy anywhere in the world when the stakes were high and the odds were long. It was the execution—no pun intended—of such missions that earned him his nickname. Now in his mid-eighties, he'd been retired for a couple of decades, but some of the organizations and countries he'd been targeted against would dearly love to get their hands on him, so he still maintains tenuous ties with his old bosses, which gives him access to some pretty neat 'toys,' that he occasionally allows me to field test for him.

I met Carlton through Quincy when I was trying to stay one step ahead of a Chinese mobster out to separate me from my head. That was also when I met Carlton's current lady friend, Margaret Sung. I never really understood how Quincy and Carlton knew each other, and had a sense it was better not to ask.

Carlton's road was so nondescript, anyone not looking for it would drive right past without seeing it, which was the idea. He didn't particularly like company. Quincy, Buster, and I were the exceptions.

Actually, calling it a road was a bit of an overstatement. It was really just a path, tire tracks pressed into the hard gray dirt, a one-lane access way wide enough for only one vehicle, with ditches to each side, the walls so sharp that it was impossible to turn around until you reached the end, in Carlton's front yard. But, like I said, unless they were looking for it, it's unlikely a casual stranger would even notice it, so any vehicle approaching the house was either expected, or invited, or an enemy. I sympathized with any enemy taking that road.

The log cabin was larger than it looked from the outside, and, with its steel reinforced roof, three-foot-thick walls, shatter resistant windows, and heavy metal doors, capable of withstanding anything less than an artillery barrage or an assault from a tank. Inside it, Carlton had state of the art monitoring equipment and an armory worthy of an infantry battalion.

As I drove slowly along the winding path, I knew that he was monitoring me every inch of the way. The path was lined with oak, maple, birch, and pine trees, back about six feet on each side, and somewhere in there were cameras capable of low-light and infrared recording and panning, all from a *Star Trek*-like console in the locked room just behind what Carlton called his sitting room. But, try as I might, I'd never been able to spot them.

The path made a gentle curve around to the right, and there, in a clearing with a hundred-meter field of fire in all directions sat Carlton's cabin. I pulled to a stop about twenty meters from the building. As usual, Carlton was standing there on his front porch waiting for me. A broad smile creased his nut brown face.

"Well, young fella," he said as I approached. "Nice seeing you again so soon."

He had a cultured southern accent that women swooned over, and as befitting his generation, was always what he termed as 'appropriately dressed' for the occasion. On the occasion of welcoming visitors, he wore blue cotton trousers with a razor sharp crease and a light blue cotton shirt open at the neck. His close cropped wavy hair was brushed tight against his skull. When I stepped up on the porch and took his hand, his grip was still firm. His dark brown eyes twinkled with just a hint of the mischief of which he was capable.

"I need to bounce something off you, and get your sage advice," I said.

I've long since stopped saying I just dropped by for a friendly visit. I'm not the 'drop by' type, and he knows it, and Carlton's better at detecting bullshit and lies than I am.

"Well, come on inside. I have a fresh pot of Colombian brewing, and with Liz at work, I have no one to share it with."

Elizabeth, a Chinatown lawyer when I first met her, had decided to reopen her practice on Ninth Street where she mostly provided assistance to new immigrants from China. This left Carlton alone during the week, and I knew he appreciated the visits.

"Sorry I don't make it out more often," I said. "You know, you should come see me at my office some time. I can show you how a modern PI works."

We both laughed at that. The only modern thing about my operation is Heather and her computer skills. Other than that, I'm about as high-tech as a character from a Mickey Spillane novel.

He pointed me to the large overstuffed sofa in the center of the room facing the door and went to the big wooden credenza to the right to pour two large mugs of coffee. The aroma of freshly brewed coffee, with just a hint of chicory, filled the room. Carlton's old school, he makes his coffee the way my grandmother taught me, with a bit of chicory to cut the bitterness. Sometimes, he adds a stick of cinnamon for flavor. He handed me a cup and took a seat on the sofa at the far end, looking at me, but positioned so he could also watch the front door and move in any direction if necessary. Like my thing about never sitting with my back to an entrance in a public place, I'm sure that habit had saved his skin on more than one occasion.

"Oh, I don't much like going into town anymore," he said after taking a sip of his coffee. "I kind of like my own company. I guess that's a bonus of getting old."

"You're not old, just vintage," I said.

He chuckled. "You're going to have to learn to lie better than that if you ever want to be in the intelligence business. Now, what's eating at your craw?"

There are a lot of things I like about Carlton, but this, I think, is the thing I like most: he knows when to cut to the chase. And, he usually has a good idea of the problem long before you know yourself, but he's pretty good at letting you think you solved it yourself. The guy's more than just a killer with a pretty face.

I gave him the rundown on the case, most of which he'd heard before at Buster's house, but I brought him up to date with the Macauley murder—I was pretty sure it was murder—and my feelings about the possible threats against Carson.

"What has me stumped," I said. "Is that neither of the women strike me as the type who'd do anyone harm. I'm pretty sure Macauley's death is somehow linked to my original case, but I can't figure out how either woman could have poisoned him."

He put his cup down and turned on the sofa cushion to face me.

"You're right that in order to poison someone, it's necessary to have physical contact, or at least access to something that will touch them, in this case some container for this herbal tea, and I believe the police are correct about it being the vehicle for the poison. But, getting such contact or access is not as hard as you might think."

"I'm not talking about the old KGB use

of poison gas darts fired from a modified umbrella," I said. "This involved getting someone to drink tea. That's pretty personal and would require getting in real close, something I don't think either of the women could do considering their relationship to the Waylon case."

"Yes, if this Macauley did in fact withhold evidence in that case, it's highly unlikely he would break bread with the man's sister or fiancée," he said. "So, that means you need to revise your list of potential suspects."

"Revise in what way?"

He shook his head. "No, I misspoke," he said. "Not so much your list of potential suspects, as your whole approach to the case."

I must have looked as confused as I felt. It was unlike Carlton to be so imprecise.

"Okay," he continued. "Let me rephrase this. You've been focusing on the fact that people like the judge and this Macauley fellow were targets because of their involvement in the Waylon case, right?"

"Well, of course."

"But, what if the reason is not the one you assume?"

I was just getting more confused.

"Now, hear me out," he said, clearly sensing my confusion. "You're assuming they're being targeted by someone who is upset about the conviction and execution of young mister Waylon, but, what if they're being targeted for a completely different reason?"

Suddenly, as if he'd just slapped me, what he was trying to say was clear. I had been focusing not just on two suspects, but one motive. What if . . .?

"Look," he continued. "When people kill for revenge, it tends to be spontaneous and messy, even when they plan it out ahead. It's the emotion involved, you see. Poison, on the other hand, is a cold and calculating way to kill someone. Except for the wife who puts rat poison in her abusive husband's food, people who use poison do it for reasons other than revenge."

"So, what I have to do is go back and deconstruct this whole case," I said. "I guess a good place to start is how in the hell someone gets a person to drink or eat digitalis."

"No, youngster, the first thing you need to do is go to school about poisons. You're thinking of digitalis in its medicinal form, but as a poison, that's not the only way it exists."

Now, I have to confess, my knowledge of poisons is so vast, you could take it, cram it in your eye, and you wouldn't even need eye drops.

"Okay, so what other form does this heart attack medicine come in?"

The look he gave me was withering. I doubt I'd have passed a class on how to poison your enemy.

"Broaden your thinking," he said. "A most common source of digitalis is the common foxglove."

"Fox what?"

"Foxglove, *digitalis purpurea*," he said. "An attractive ornamental flower found in many gardens. It's prized for its beautiful blossoms, shaped like tiny, inverted champagne glasses, their purple, pink, white, and yellow colors add a delightful accent to any garden."

I'm not much for gardening. Or any other kind of yard work for that matter. Except for the area right around the house and barn—and that to get rid of possible nesting places for snakes—I let the deer take care of my grass cutting. His description of foxglove, though, seemed familiar for some reason.

"So, you get digitalis poison from the flowers of this plant?"

"No, my boy, you get it from just about any part of this plant. Everything about it is toxic: roots, sap, flowers, pollen, leaves, seeds—they're all toxic, even when dried. You can get a nasty dose of digitalis from just rubbing against the stalks or leaves, and only five grams of dried digitalis can kill you."

I couldn't really picture five grams, but I knew it was a pretty small amount. At a mere 28 grams in an ounce, five grams would be about one-third of a pint. I wasn't sure how you could camouflage that in tea, though.

"That seems like a lot of poison to pour down someone's throat," I said, picturing a third of a pint.

"Not really," he said. "Tea made from foxglove is sometimes mistaken for that made from comfrey, a plant that's harmless, and people have accidentally poisoned themselves. The taste of the digitalis can be masked with chamomile or honey, so you could give someone a cup or glass of foxglove tea, and they might just drink the whole thing."

"Yeah, but wouldn't they start getting sick before drinking that much?"

He smiled; a vulpine smile that gave me shivers.

"Not really. It takes a few minutes for it to take effect, and at first the symptoms are feeling faint and maybe vomiting—oh, and the blood pressure drops. A person wouldn't necessarily connect them with the tea. If, however, there's a severe drop in blood pressure, they're likely to faint, and if they don't get immediate medical care to flush the poison from their system, they're very likely to expire."

Sounded like it came right out of the spy training manual, the one where civilian casualties are collateral damage and assassination is termination with extreme prejudice. But, it did put a whole new light on my case.

"So, the person who did this would likely be known and trusted by the victim."

"Most likely," he said.

TWENTY-SEVEN

On the way back to the office I remembered why Carlton's description of the foxglove plant seemed familiar. He'd described the plant I'd seen in the glass case at Witch's Brew.

That little bit of news didn't do much for my list of potential suspects.

"Heather," I said as I walked through the door. "I need you to do some serious research on foxglove."

She looked up from what she was doing.

"Why would anyone want to put gloves on a fox?"

"No, not fox-space-glove as in gloves for a fix, but foxglove the plant."

Her eyebrows rose a good half inch.

"Why on earth to you want to know anything about a plant?"

I explained what Carlton had told me. "I need to know just how toxic it is, what ways it can be administered, the whole shooting match."

She stared at me with her mouth open. Then she snapped it shut.

"Well," I said. "What are you waiting

for?"

She turned her attention to her computer, and tapped on the keys. Then, she stared down at the screen.

"Oh, my goodness," she said.

I walked over and looked over her shoulder at the screen.

"Wow," I said.

The picture on the screen was in full color. The foxglove is a beautiful flower. I can see why people like them in their gardens. But then I read the text underneath the picture. Holy crap! This beautiful flower is the Mata Hari of the plant world; it's Lucretia Borgia of the garden. This is one plant you don't want to mess with unless you know what you're doing.

I wondered if Penelope Payton knew what she was doing.

TWENTY-EIGHT

I sat at my desk with my head cupped in my hands, and stared at the wall in front of me.

I often have cases where I have no suspects, and I have to look at everyone involved to see who benefits most. In this case, I had two prime suspects, neither of whom I wanted to believe capable of anything really serious, but both with the means and motive to kill Thomas Macauley, and perhaps go after Isaac Carson. What I was lacking was proof that either had the opportunity.

I had Heather's list of names and my notes on the desk between my elbows. I looked down at them, hoping some insight would leap off one of the pages. Nothing happened.

Then, Carlton Raine's words popped into my consciousness, "But, what if the reason is not the one you assume?" I've heard that really creative writers play the 'what if' game, asking 'what if?' about the most outlandish things to get their creative juices flowing. His question had been so simple, and I'd played along, but mentally had clung to the same assumption I'd started with. This case was about someone wanting vengeance for Henry Waylon's death. What if that wasn't the reason?

I snatched my notes off the desk and crumbled the sheet of paper. After dropping it into the trash can behind my desk, I took a clean sheet and laid it on the desk next to the list of names.

Taking out my pen, I wrote across the top of the sheet,

Why would someone want Thomas Macauley dead?

I put the pen down and stared at the sentence, letting my mind roam free. There are a number of motives for murder. I listed the main ones that I thought might be in play here,

Why would someone want Thomas Macauley dead?
1. Money – theft or murder for hire
2. Revenge – for Henry Waylon's death?
3. To cover up a crime – victim's withholding of evidence?

While I couldn't completely rule out motive number 1; there'd been no indication of a robbery, but Macauley had prosecuted a few mobsters in his time; it didn't seem likely. I'd just listed it first because it was the first that had popped into my mind. The second motive seemed most likely, but given the rumor that Macauley had withheld important evidence, an ethical lapse if not a crime, it was likely that someone else knew about it, and was afraid of being exposed, I couldn't afford to ignore motive three.

Revenge clearly left Yolanda and Penelope on the list of suspects, but if the ADA was killed to cover up a crime, I needed to look for another suspect. A good one, for my money, was Allan Bavan. Sure, he'd acted scared the last time I visited him on his boat, but he could have been faking. The man was an experienced detective who would know how to put on an act to fool a suspect. I would have to have Heather take a much closer look at him. If he was involved in the evidence tampering, he'd certainly have a motive for shutting Macauley up, and as a former cop, he'd have no problem getting close to the man. The flaw in my argument, though, was means. For all his cop skills, I didn't see him having the intelligence to use an exotic poison like digitalis to kill a man.

Then, I had another thought,

Why would someone want Thomas Macauley dead?
1. *Money – theft or murder for hire*
2. *Revenge – for Henry Waylon's death?*
3. *To cover up a crime – victim's withholding of evidence?*

Is the threat against Isaac Carson real or a red herring?

So far no one had made a move on the judge. In fact, the only victim was Thomas Macauley. What if the threat to the judge was meant to misdirect any investigation to cover up Macauley's murder? What if he was the *only* intended victim?

As I thought that, my eye fell on

Heather's list.

Henry Waylon – convicted of rape/murder '92 (22), executed '02(32)
Colleen Adamson – rape/murder victim '92.(15)
Malcolm Jenkins – Waylon's lawyer/public defender
Thomas Macauley – assistant DA/prosecutor *Deceased, heart failure?*
Isaac P. Carson – presiding judge
Allan Bavan – lead detective on Waylon's case
Yolanda Waylon – Henry's sister (25)
Penelope Payton – Henry's girlfriend (30)
Charles Armstrong – Henry's classmate/roommate (32)
Michael Fletcher – Henry's classmate/roommate (34)
Jurors:
Gunther Weiss – foreman, recently deceased (72) *Heart failure*
Alison Morgan (50)
Lane Coltrane (60)
Joseph Leslie (68), *Recently deceased, heart failure*
William Gordon (65)
Melvin Pettigrew (60)
Samuel Carter (61)
Edgar Melton (62)
Bettina Adams (60)
Lance Woodson (52)
Ben Johnson (67)
Raymond Harris (62)

Macauley death ruled possible homicide by police.

Heather had annotated the list in her precise hand writing, probably during one of my absences from the office. As I stared at it, my eyes were drawn to the two jurors. Sure, they were elderly men, and their deaths hadn't aroused any suspicion, but really, three people connected to the Waylon case, all dying within a few days of each other of the same cause?

My mind was screaming, 'no way! That is just *too* much coincidence. There was something else going on here. But, what?

I had a feeling, an itching at the base of my skull; that this wasn't over, not by a long shot. Call it intuition, call it gut feeling; call it whatever the hell you want, but I was pretty sure we hadn't seen the last corpse. I was also pretty sure that Waylon's sister wasn't the killer, and was reasonably sure his former fiancée was also innocent.

Now, all I had to do was find the real killer before too many more people died.

TWENTY-NINE

On Friday morning, as I sat behind my desk glancing at my watch, seeing that it was approaching lunch time, my mind was still swimming with the possibilities that I'd so clearly seen the day before. Now, though, the water through they swam was decidedly murky. One part of my brain was working the case, while the other part was thinking that the day was almost half over, and I had a weekend ahead of me, two days when I planned to do nothing but cuddle with Sandra.

I'd just about decided to knock off early for lunch, and maybe even for the day, when the phone rang. It was Buster.

"Morning, bro," he said in that booming voice of his as soon as I said hello. "You sitting down?"

"I'm in my office, what else would I be doing?"

"Just wanted to make sure," he said. He didn't sound like he was joking.

My antenna went up. Buster, though he liked to yank my chain on occasion, wasn't one for phone pranks.

"Okay, pal, I'm sitting, what's up?"

"I just finished a crime scene that I thought you'd be interested in knowing about," he said. "Charles Armstrong, the guy you said was Henry Waylon's roommate, was just found dead in his apartment."

"I'm guessing death was not from natural causes."

"How'd you guess?

I had to laugh.

"A DC homicide detective wouldn't be calling me about an accident," I said.

"Well, I reckon that must be why you collect them big PI fees. You're right, it wasn't an accident. In fact, so far it looks just like that dude over in Arlington, Macauley. We're still waiting for the ME report, but the conditions when the guy's body was found look the same, and the doc on scene said it looked like he died between ten and midnight last night."

This was getting, as Alice said in *Behind the Looking Glass*, curiouser and curiouser. This was now definitely out of 'coincidence' territory.

"The same M.O. means it's likely the same killer," I said. "But, Armstrong doesn't fit the victim profile. He was a friend of Henry Waylon."

"Yeah, but don't forget, he didn't give him an alibi."

I was beginning not to like where I thought he was going.

"There's something you're on the verge of not telling me, Buster. Come on, out with it."

He made a growling noise. It reverberated inside my head.

"Look, bro, if my captain knew I was talking to you about this case, he'd have my balls, so you got to be cool about this, okay?"

"Discretion is my middle name," I said.

"Bullshit, I know your middle name's Einstein. Just be careful with what you do with what I'm about to tell you."

I would never deliberately do anything to get Buster in trouble. I've inadvertently gotten him into trouble in the past, but all with the best of intentions.

"You got my promise, amigo. I will not let anyone know you talked to me."

"And, you ain't gonna do nothing that'll get me in trouble?"

"You know I'll do my best."

"Shit, I guess that's the best I'm gonna get out of you." He made that growling sound again. "Look, everyone in the precinct knows the history of the Waylon case, and how the kid's sister went ballistic in the courtroom when he was sentenced. There's nothing yet that ties her to the scene here, but pretty soon, I'm gonna have to pull her in for questioning."

Shit's right. I didn't see her as a good suspect in Macauley's death, and even less did I think she'd kill her brother's roommate. It didn't make sense.

"My gut's telling me that it's very likely the same person killed both men," I said.

"Me too, and that's what the captain's telling the cops over the river. They're gonna be looking a little closer at her for the Macauley killing."

"Why the hell would you guys do that?"

"Hey, don't shoot the messenger, bro," he said. "If we do decide to bring her in, we'll need them to pick her up for us. It's standard procedure. You know that."

I knew that. I didn't like it, because I thought they were on the wrong track, but I knew he was following correct procedure. It's just that the correct procedure was going to get the wrong person caught up in the justice system yet again.

"Yeah, I know. Sorry I snapped at you. Anything else?"

"No, just wanted to let you know. I know she's involved in the case you're working on. In fact, from everything you told me, I'd think she'd be your number one suspect for the threatening note against you-know-who."

I wasn't ready to share my new theory. I didn't have anything but a gut feeling yet, anyway.

"Well, she is on a long list of people with connections to the Waylon case," I said. "She's not my main suspect, though."

"Can you tell me who is?"

"Not right now I can't."

"Can't or won't?"

"Come on, Buster, you know me," I said. "If I know the identity of a criminal, I'd share it with the police." I decided to feed him a little. "The problem is, right now I don't really have a good suspect. I keep running down a lot of blind alleys."

"I know you and your blind alleys. Are these leading to someone or away from someone?"

"They're just blind alleys." I decided to be a bit more up front with him. After all, we'd been friends for a long time. "There's something about Clayburn's murder that bothers me, but I can't put my finger on it."

"Something like what?" I couldn't tell if he was taking the bait or being polite, or if it was just a cop's inquisitiveness.

"Well, I talked to Blood about it, and he and I both agree that it looked to cold and calculating to fit the profile of anyone I know in this case yet."

There was a long pause. I could hear him breathing.

"Come on, bro," he said finally. "You sure you're not just reacting to the fact that Yolanda Waylon's a veteran?"

"How did you--"

"Hey, man, I graduated from the police academy at the top of my class," he said. Then he laughed. "The first thing I do is run a quick background check on a . . . person of interest."

If he'd done that, he would know she had a medical lab background in the army, he would know she worked for a pharmaceutical company, and he'd pretty quickly find out that she had access to digitalis. I hated what I was about to do, but I needed time to see if my new theory about things was valid.

"Well, I'll admit that her being a veteran makes me a bit more sympathetic." True. "And, her background and current employment means I can't take her off my suspect list, either for threatening the judge or offing Macauley." Partially true. I didn't see her as a killer. "Same thing goes for Waylon's former fiancée, Penelope Payton." Not really true, except for those plants in her shop. "She was pretty devastated when he was convicted, and is still carrying a torch for him." Sorry, Penelope, but it's all in a good cause. "So, amigo, you can see my dilemma? I have two people with plenty of motive—except in Armstrong's case. I think the same person who killed Macauley probably killed him, given the M.O., but I can't figure out the motive." Sorry, Buster, but if I'm right, you'll forgive me later.

"The fiancée? Damn, I hadn't thought about her," he said. "I better do some more digging before we move on Waylon. Thanks, bro. You probably saved us from making a big mistake."

As I broke the connection, I crossed my fingers. I was hoping that I wasn't making a big mistake.

THIRTY

What I was about to do was pretty close to the line of interfering with a police investigation.

I drove across the river to MedGen. After finding a slot in the parking lot behind the building, I made my way back around front, went inside and asked the receptionist if I could see Yolanda Waylon.

I only had to wait five minutes for her to show up.

"Mr. Pennyback," she said. "What more can I do to help you?"

She had a nice smile. I just couldn't see her as a murderer.

"Ms. Waylon, do you have a few minutes, and is there somewhere more private than this where we can talk?"

Her brow wrinkled, and then just as quickly smoothed.

"Yeah, I suppose so," she said. "I was about to take my break anyway. You see the fountain out front? The one with all the hedges around it. There's benches in there. I like to sit out there sometimes and watch the butterflies."

Without waiting for my acknowledgment, she headed for the exit.

She led me to a little cul de sac in the shrubbery surrounding the fountain in front of the building. It contained a two-person marble bench with an urn set in the concrete next to it, and was shaded by the enveloping shrubs.

"This is where people take their smoke breaks," she said. "I don't smoke, but I like coming here just to relax and get away from the sterile smell of the lab."

She motioned for me to sit, and as she sat, I noticed that she swayed. When she looked up, for the first time I saw that her face was a bit puffy, and that she had bags under her eyes.

"You look beat," I said.

I felt a tug of apprehension, wondering if she was so tired because sometime between ten and midnight she was busy killing Charles Armstrong.

"I am," she said. "My section of the lab's been at it since noon yesterday. We have this experiment running that has to be constantly monitored."

"You've been here since noon yesterday?"

She gave me a funny look.

"No, I've been here since eight yesterday. And, I feel like shit. Too much coffee and food from Mickey D's, has given me a headache and a major league case of gas."

I let out a breath, and the muscles in my body, tensed when I noticed her condition, relaxed.

"Why do you ask?" she asked. Her

214

eyebrows came together, curling up at the point where they met.

"You were here between, say, nine and one this morning, right?" I added an hour front and back for a buffer. "And, someone else can verify that?"

She looked confused.

"Yeah . . . plus, we videotape what's going on in the lab. It's mainly for insurance coverage . . . you know, in case of a lab accident. What's going on? Why are you asking me this?"

I knew I'd be stepping over the line, but if she was telling me the truth—and my bullshit meter told me she was—she had an iron-clad alibi.

I told her about Armstrong. Her hands went to her mouth. Tears welled up in her eyes.

"N-no, that can't be," she said, sobbing. "I d-didn't know him well. After the trial I didn't want to have anything to do with anyone from that school, and then I went into the army. But, I remember Henry always talking about him, and how they were like brothers. I met him a couple of times. He was such a gentle sweet person. Who would want to kill him?"

"That's what I'm planning to find out." I then told her about Macauley, and my theory that the same person who killed Armstrong also killed him.

Her eyebrows did that 'meet in the middle' thing again, and she stared at me through narrowed slits.

"Wait a minute! You were thinking I might have killed Armstrong, weren't you?"

"No, I wasn't," I said. "In fact, I was

convinced you didn't. If I hadn't thought you were innocent, I'd never have come here and told you." That much was true. It was time, though, to see how accurate my instincts were. "What I thought you were guilty of was sending a threatening note to Isaac Carson, the judge in your brother's case. But now, I'm convinced you didn't do that either."

She looked at me with an expression that I imagine was the same one she used looking at a bug under a microscope. Then, she leaned back and laughed.

"I guess I can see how you'd think that. I did pitch quite a hissy fit in the courtroom. And, I guess I might have sounded threatening at the time. But, shit, I was only fifteen, and that son of a bitch had just sentenced my brother to die, so yeah, I blew a gasket. But, I've matured a lot since then. If the army taught me one thing, it's the importance of not dwelling on things in the past, or things that you have no control over. Say, why do the cops think I might have killed Chuck Armstrong?"

I explained the suspected cause of death in both cases, and the fact that the cops had learned that she worked with digitalis in her job.

"High levels of digitalis were found in Macauley's body, and I suspect they'll find the same in Armstrong's."

"Yeah, I can see how they might jump to that conclusion," she said. "But, I can assure you, substances like digitalis are tightly controlled around here. Everyone working in the lab is scrubbed and examined thoroughly after leaving the lab. The only way you could sneak that shit out is to swallow it, and if you know anything about digitalis, you know that's a non-starter."

I had to laugh. Here I'd just told her the police suspected her of murder—maybe double murder—and, that I'd suspected her of . . . well, whatever you call it when someone sends threats—maybe assault. I'm sure there's some law somewhere against it. But, she was able to process all that, and make light of it. The army had trained her well. She'd gone in an angry, rebellious teenager, and come out a woman—a beautiful, well-balanced woman.

"Okay," I said. "So, you and I know you're innocent, and you're in the clear for Armstrong's death. Now, all I have to do is find the real killer."

"Isn't that a job for the police?"

"Yeah, but the wheels of justice turn slow at the best of times. The cops will waste time chasing useless leads and focusing on the wrong people. In the meantime, our killer just might be getting ready to strike again."

She laid a hand on my knee and smiled.

"I got a feeling you're just the man for the job. You remind me of some of the better commanders I had in the army. Well, good luck. Now, if you don't mind, I have a few more hours and then I can go home and get some sack time."

I sat there for a while after she walked away. Five or six Monarch butterflies were swarming around a plant with large white flowers off to the left. I watched them for a while. Then, I got up and headed back to my care.

One down, one to go—and, one killer to catch.

THIRTY-ONE

When I got back to the office, Heather was leafing through a thick stack of documents.

"What you got there, kid?" I asked.

She put a finger on a page to mark her spot and looked up at me. She had a broad smile on her face.

"Malcolm Jenkins sent over copies of the Waylon trial transcripts," she said. "He said maybe we could spot something in them that he missed. He feels awful that he didn't do a better job of representing Henry Waylon."

I grabbed the visitor's chair and scooted in beside her so that we both could read at the same time.

IN THE CIRCUIT COURT

OF THE COMMONWEALTH OF VIRGINIA

DISTRICT 17

AT ARLINGTON

COMMONWEALTH OF VIRGINIA,

Plaintiff,

v.

HENRY L. WAYLON,

Defendant.

NO. FM-11-92-10
Arlington, Virginia, October 9, 1992

BEFORE: THE HONORABLE ISAAC P.
CARSON, DISTRICT JUDGE

The first thing I noticed was that the trial started within three months of Waylon's arrest, which must be some kind of record in the criminal justice system. After the header information, there was a lot of legal mumbo jumbo that I guessed was boilerplate information included on all court transcripts. I stopped and whistled when I got to the part that detailed the charges against the defendant: Aggravated Assault, Unlawful Detention, Aggravated Rape, and Murder during the Commission of a Felony.

"I know what you're looking at," Heather said. "I called Malcolm after the service dropped this off, and asked about that myself. He said he didn't learn it until after the trial concluded, but this was Macauley's tactic. He'd pile on as many charges as possible, certain that he'd get the defendant convicted on at least one of them. In this case, the aggravated assault charge alone would have gotten him up to twenty years. It was the final charge, though, that carried the death penalty, and to Malcolm's surprise, the jury found him guilty on all charges."

"Sort of like being stoned," I said. "One stone might not kill you, but if you're buried under several hundred pounds of stones, you'll suffocate."

"Well, this guy Macauley loved to suffocate defendants according to Malcolm."

She laughed. I laughed, but I wasn't actually feeling the humor. My mind was on how I would approach my next meeting with Penelope Payton, now that Yolanda Waylon was no longer a suspect in my opinion.

Heather flipped the pages quickly as we skimmed the first fifteen pages of the transcript. It was taken up with the court being called to order, reading of the charges, and introduction of the lawyers; Thomas Macauley representing the plaintiff, the Commonwealth of Virginia, and Malcolm Jenkins for the defense. The defendant was asked for his plea, which his attorney stated was Not Guilty. The prosecution made the first opening statement, basically stating that the state would show that the defendant, Henry Waylon had met the victim, Colleen Adamson, at the Red Bull Lounge in Arlington on the night of June 18, 1992, and that said defendant had lured the victim to a secluded spot at the base of Key Bridge on the Virginia side, where he raped and then strangled her. In Jenkins' opening statement, he pointed out that the state's case was based entirely on circumstantial evidence, and that there was no physical evidence linking his client to the victim, other than the fact that *she* had been seen talking to him.

The prosecution got to present its case first, which consisted of a lengthy appearance by Allan Bavan, the detective in charge of the investigation. He identified himself and stated that he'd been called to the scene shortly after the body had been discovered by a local resident walking his dog, at around 6:00 am. The body had been partially concealed in the rough underbrush at the base of one of the bridge pilings. He then described the process of identifying the victim, and learning from her parents that she often hung out in the bars in and around Rosslyn. A canvas of the bars led him to the Red Bull, where the bartender remembered seeing a young woman fitting her description talking to a young black man and two young white men. A check of the credit card receipts led to the identification of Michael Fletcher as one of the white men. Checking with the credit card company, Bavan got Fletcher's address in DC, and, in the company of two officers from DC Metro Police, went there, where he also found Charles Armstrong and Henry Waylon.

Fletcher and Armstrong were interviewed first, and confirmed that they had been at the Red Bull in the company of Waylon. At first, they didn't know where he was, but when they checked his bedroom, they found him fully dressed, lying on top of the bed covers. He seemed disoriented, his clothing was disheveled, and there were dirt stains on the knees of his trousers. He also had bruises on the palms of his hands. He couldn't explain the stains or the injuries. He remembered being at the Red Bull, and the young woman who had talked to him and his friends. He said that he'd begun feeling ill, so he'd gone outside the bar to get some air. He then claimed that the next thing he remembered was waking up lying across his bed.

Bavan then had the DC cops take him into custody and transport him to Arlington, where he was further questioned. His inability to explain where he'd been from the time he left the bar until he was found in his bedroom, along with the physical evidence on his clothing and body were considered sufficient to arrest him on suspicion. Three days later, the DA's office brought formal charges.

Bavan was followed by a representative of the ME's office who described the body of Colleen Adamson, the scene where it was found, the cause of death—manual strangulation—the fact that she'd been sexually assaulted ante-mortem, and that her time of death was between 10:30 pm and midnight.

The bartender followed the ME, and he pointed at Henry Waylon, identifying him as the young black man to whom the victim had been talking. He said that he hadn't seen either of them after 10:00 pm.

It was on page sixteen that the transcript got interesting. Charles Armstrong was called as a witness for the prosecution. He took the oath, and identified himself as a classmate and roommate of the defendant.

CHARLES GABRIEL ARMSTRONG, called as a witness for the Plaintiff,
having been first duly sworn, was examined and testified as
follows:

DIRECT EXAMINATION

MR. MACAULEY:

Q: Please state your name, address and occupation for the record.

A: Charles Gabriel Armstrong, I live at 1872 Twenty-First Street
Washington, DC, and I'm a student at George Washington
University.

Q: Are you acquainted with the defendant, Henry Waylon?

A: Yes.

Q: What is the nature of your relationship with Mr. Waylon?

A: We share an apartment, and are classmates in the pre-med
program at George Washington.

Q: How long have you known the defendant?

A: Since we were freshmen, three years now.

Q: Now, Mr. Armstrong, can you tell us what happened on the night
of June 18 of this year?

A: Well, Henry and Mike, that's our other roommate Michael
Fletcher, had just gotten words that we'd done well on our final
exams, so we decided to go out and celebrate. We went first to M
Street in Georgetown, and then decided to walk across Key Bridge
to Arlington and try some of the places over there.

Q: And, you ended up at the Red Bull

Lounge.

MR. JENKINS: Objection, your honor, leading the witness.

THE COURT: Sustained. Mr. Macauley, please restate your
question.

MR. MACAULEY: Yes, your honor, my apologies.

Q: Mr. Armstrong, where in Arlington did you go?

A: We went to the Red Bull Lounge on Wilson Boulevard.
Mike had heard that it was a happening place.

Q: Yes, now, what happened after you arrived at the Red Bull?

A: We had a few drinks. I don't recall how many. Shortly after we
arrived this girl started talking to us, well, mostly talking to Henry.

Q: Can you tell us who this girl was?

A: Well, I didn't know her name at the time. I learned later that
she was Colleen Adamson. Anyway, she starts talking to us, er,
Henry, but he didn't really want to talk to her.

MR. MACAULEY: Your honor, move to strike the last sentence.
Goes to the defendant's state of mind.

THE COURT: Sustained. Jury will disregard any statement about
What the defendant might have been thinking.

Q: Now, Mr. Armstrong, you say the victim was talking to the
defendant. What happened next?

A: Well, around 10:00, I think, it was right after Mike had
bought a round, Henry said he wasn't feeling well, and
he was going out to get some fresh air. We kept drinking,
and I guess I didn't notice that Henry didn't come back.
When I did, I guess I assumed he wanted to get away from
that girl, Colleen, you know.

Q: Mr. Armstrong, was Ms. Adamson attractive?

A: Uh, yeah, I guess so.

Q: A beautiful, young blonde woman, in fact. And,
you're trying to tell the court that the defendant was
not attracted to her?

A: Well, Henry already has a girlfriend. In fact,
he's engaged.

Q: Ah, yes, to a Penelope Payton, a fellow student.
Miss Payton is also an attractive blonde, right?

A: Uh, yeah.

Q: So, the defendant, Henry Waylon seems to have
a thing for blondes, wouldn't you say?

MR. JENKINS: Your honor, I object in the strongest
terms to this blatant attempt to smear my client.

THE COURT: Sustained. Mr. Macauley, you're an
experienced officer of the court who should know
better. The jury will disregard this entire exchange.

MR. MACAULEY: Again, my apologies, your
Honor. I humbly withdraw that question. I have
one final question for this witness.

Q: Mr. Armstrong, you say the defendant, Henry Waylon,
didn't return to the Red Bull? When did you see him
next, and where did Ms. Adamson go?

A: The next time I saw Henry was at the apartment
the next day when the police came. As for the girl,
Ms. Adamson, I don't know where she went. I just
noticed that after Henry left, she wasn't there any more.

MR. MACAULEY: I have no further questions for
this witness.

THE COURT: Mr. Jenkins, do you wish to cross
examine the witness?

MR. JENKINS: No, your honor.

Macauley's examination of Charles Armstrong had been classic. He'd done a masterful job of planting in the jury's mind a picture of a young black man with a taste for young white girls—without ever once having to say it directly. And, while his innuendo had been admonished by the judge, and the jury had been instructed to disregard it, it had been planted in their minds, and even though they would probably swear it had no bearing on their subsequent verdict, it couldn't help but color everything else presented during the trial.

The next witness was one of the waitresses from the Red Bull, who testified that she'd seen the victim talking to the defendant, that both of them seem to have disappeared around 10:00 pm—she remembered the time, because she'd just come back inside from a smoke break at the rear of the building.

For his final witness, Macauley had called Michael Fletcher. When I saw the name, I thought it strange that he wouldn't have called Fletcher immediately after Armstrong because of their relationship, until I got to the part about events just prior to Waylon leaving the bar.

Q: Mr. Fletcher, you've said that Ms. Adamson was, in
our words, coming on to, Mr. Waylon. How did he
respond to her
overtures?

A: He's a man, and she's, er, she was, a pretty girl.
How do you
think he responded?

Q: You'll need to be a bit more specific for the jury,
Mr. Fletcher.

A: He was, er, aroused, I guess you could say. I
mean, she was
rubbing her breasts against his arm, and her, you-
know-what
against his legs. I could see that he was, er, aroused.

Q: But, your roommate, Mr. Armstrong said he was

trying
to ignore her.

A: He might have been at first, but not just before he left. Chuck
had had a few too many, and besides, I was standing between
them, so he might not have seen what I saw.

Q: So, what happened next.

A: Well, around ten, Henry said he wasn't feeling well, and
that he was going outside for some air, and he and the girl
left.

Q: They left together?

A: Oh no, not together. He left first, and then right away
she left.

MR. MACAULEY: I have no further questions of this witness, your honor.

THE COURT: Mr. Jenkins, do you wish to cross examine the witness?

MR. JENKINS: Yes, I do, your honor.

CROSS EXAMINATION:

Q: Mr. Fletcher, did you see my client and Ms. Adamson leave the
bar together?

A: No, I didn't see them leave together.

The rest of the transcript was pretty boring. The prosecution rested its case after Fletcher's testimony. I had to give Jenkins credit for making an effort, although there was little he could do against a skillful manipulator like Macauley. During the defense's presentation, he recalled Armstrong and Fletcher to the stand and questioned them as hostile witnesses, but they essentially repeated the same stories. Henry Waylon didn't testify in his own defense, which Quincy assures me is most often the best strategy, but his inability—probably seen by the jury as evasiveness—to remember anything from the time he left the bar, stood unanswered. He was damned if he did and double-damned when he didn't. During closing testimony, the prosecution brought that up several times—that refusal to testify to try and set the record straight. Jenkins' closing statement was impassioned, focusing on the circumstantial nature of the state's case, but ultimately, to no avail. The jury was only out six hours before returning with guilty verdicts on all counts.

Judge Isaac P. Carson, thanked the jury for their service and dismissed them, stated that sentencing would be a week later, remanded Henry Waylon into the custody of the bailiff to be taken back to his cell, and adjourned court, beginning a futile ten-year wait for Waylon as appeal after appeal was denied until his final date with the needle in the execution chamber at Greenville Correctional Facility in Jarratt, Virginia.

For a public defender, short on funds at the best of times, Jenkins had done a lot for Waylon, much of it, I learned from Heather, on his own time and his own dime after he left the public defenders office. I'm sure he'd read these transcripts over and over, looking for some small point upon which to base an appeal. But, he'd missed it.

I hadn't, though. Maybe it was due to my

not having been involved in the trial, so I read it without expecting to see anything. But, when I read Fletcher's testimony, and went back and compared it to Armstrong's, it jumped off the page at me.

I knew who had raped and killed Colleen Adamson. The same person who'd killed Thomas Macauley and Charles Armstrong, and probably sent the threatening note to Judge Isaac Carson. I had a glimmer of an idea about the motive, and knew he had the means. I only had to figure out how he got the opportunity.

THIRTY-TWO

To a casual reader, Michael Fletcher's testimony would seem innocent enough. He came off as an honest man, giving his recollection of events—nothing there that blatantly accused his former roommate of the crime for which he was being tried.

It was the subtle differences, though, between his recollection and that of Charles Armstrong, differences that someone too familiar with the trial might not notice.

Fletcher hadn't mentioned that he was the one who bought the drinks just before Waylon complained of dizziness and left the bar. Armstrong had not only said that in his testimony, but had mentioned it to me when I met him. Funny how the mind works—well, it's funny at least how *my* mind works. His omission of that simple fact set me to thinking. Fletcher was a medical student. He'd know how chemicals worked, and he might have access to them—chemicals that skew perception, make people dizzy, like the popular date rape drugs, of which there are many. It would've been easy for him to slip something into Waylon's drink. That would explain Waylon's inability to recall anything after leaving the bar.

In addition to that, there were Penelope Payton's comments about Fletcher, as well as his own demeanor when I spoke to him. In other words, there was something off about the man. I'd just failed to pick it up at first.

For whatever reason, my mind had jumped to the conclusion, no conviction, that it was Michael Fletcher who had raped and killed Colleen Adamson, and that it was Fletcher who had poisoned Thomas Macauley and Charles Armstrong. I was also convinced that Allan Bavan would be next on Fletcher's hit list.

But, I needed more than this flash of inspiration. I needed some hard evidence.

I slapped a hand on the transcript, causing Heather to push her chair back and look at me with wide eyes.

"What the-"

"Sorry," I said. "But, I need you to do something for me. Get the number of this Innocence Project, and get me someone on the line."

Heather's quick on the uptake. She knows that when I get that look in my eye, and start issuing orders without explanation, I'm on to something. Hell, for all I know, she'd probably seen the same thing I'd seen, and come to the same conclusion.

She had an Innocence Project representative on the phone within ten minutes.

"Felicity Nugent, deputy coordinator,

Innocence Project," a voice with a New England accent said into my ear. "How may I help you?"

"Ms. Nugent, my name's Al Pennyback, I'm a private investigator working on a case related to the conviction of Henry Waylon."

I heard a sharp intake of breath.

"Oh, yes. Poor Mr. Waylon," she said. "It was so tragic that we didn't get that case early enough to allow us to do our analysis in time to get a stay of execution. What is it you'd like to know?"

"Just a couple questions," I said. "First, who referred the case to you?"

"Just a moment, let me look." There was the sound of papers rustling. "Yes, here it is; Mr. Waylon's case was referred to us by Charles Armstrong. I understand that he was a college classmate."

"That's correct. Now, according to the news reports, your analysis concluded that Henry Waylon could not have been involved in the crime. What led you to that conclusion?"

"Well, I must be specific. Our analysis didn't conclude that he didn't commit the crime. The media interpreted it that way. Our tests, though, did show that the physical evidence, especially the DNA, found at the scene, was not related to Henry Waylon."

This was sounding interesting. "Just how did you come to that conclusion?" I asked.

"Because all of the DNA was from a single individual, a male of northern European ancestry. In other words, the DNA at the scene was from a white male, not from an African-American."

Bingo!

"One more question, Ms. Nugent. Do you happen to know the chain of custody of the evidence in question?"

"Yes, as a matter of fact," she said. "It was annotated on the report we got when we received the evidence. It was collected at the scene the morning the body was found, sent to the crime lab, and then returned to the evidence locker, all in a matter of ten days."

So, the crime lab had placed a white male at the scene within ten days of the crime, and months before the trial. There was no way Macauley hadn't known of it, and a good chance that Bavan knew as well. The fuckers had railroaded an innocent man. Sent him to his death, knowing that he was innocent, or at least knowing that there was a reasonable doubt, had the defense had access to that crucial bit of evidence. I had one more question.

"Ms. Nugent, did the police ever identify the person to whom this DNA belonged?"

"No, not as far as I know. You must remember, though, the use of DNA was still rather rudimentary back then. Unless they happened to have a suspect in mind from whom to take a sample for comparison, it's unlikely they'd be able to pinpoint a specific person."

I just happened to have a suspect in mind, and at that point I would have liked to personally rip off a piece of his flesh for comparison. Of course, as an officer of the court, and not wanting to have my license yanked, I wouldn't do that.

I would have to be more subtle.

I thanked Ms. Nugent for her help and rang off.

To a casual reader, Michael Fletcher's testimony would seem innocent enough. He came off as an honest man, giving his recollection of events—nothing there that blatantly accused his former roommate of the crime for which he was being tried.

It was the subtle differences, though, between his recollection and that of Charles Armstrong, differences that someone too familiar with the trial might not notice.

Fletcher hadn't mentioned that he was the one who bought the drinks just before Waylon complained of dizziness and left the bar. Armstrong had not only said that in his testimony, but had mentioned it to me when I met him. Funny how the mind works—well, it's funny at least how *my* mind works. His omission of that simple fact set me to thinking. Fletcher was a medical student. He'd know how chemicals worked, and he might have access to them—chemicals that skew perception, make people dizzy, like the popular date rape drugs, of which there are many. It would've been easy for him to slip something into Waylon's drink. That would explain Waylon's inability to recall anything after leaving the bar.

In addition to that, there were Penelope Payton's comments about Fletcher, as well as his own demeanor when I spoke to him. In other words, there was something off about the man. I'd just failed to pick it up at first.

For whatever reason, my mind had jumped to the conclusion, no conviction, that it was Michael Fletcher who had raped and killed Colleen Adamson, and that it was Fletcher who had poisoned Thomas Macauley and Charles Armstrong. I was also convinced that Allan Bavan would be next on Fletcher's hit list.

But, I needed more than this flash of inspiration. I needed some hard evidence.

I slapped a hand on the transcript, causing Heather to push her chair back and look at me with wide eyes.

"What the-"

"Sorry," I said. "But, I need you to do something for me. Get the number of this Innocence Project, and get me someone on the line."

Heather's quick on the uptake. She knows that when I get that look in my eye, and start issuing orders without explanation, I'm on to something. Hell, for all I know, she'd probably seen the same thing I'd seen, and come to the same conclusion.

She had an Innocence Project representative on the phone within ten minutes.

"Felicity Nugent, deputy coordinator, Innocence Project," a voice with a New England accent said into my ear. "How may I help you?"

"Ms. Nugent, my name's Al Pennyback, I'm a private investigator working on a case related to the conviction of Henry Waylon."

I heard a sharp intake of breath.

"Oh, yes. Poor Mr. Waylon," she said. "It was so tragic that we didn't get that case early enough to allow us to do our analysis in time to get a stay of execution. What is it you'd like to know?"

"Just a couple questions," I said. "First, who referred the case to you?"

"Just a moment, let me look." There was the sound of papers rustling. "Yes, here it is;

Mr. Waylon's case was referred to us by Charles Armstrong. I understand that he was a college classmate."

"That's correct. Now, according to the news reports, your analysis concluded that Henry Waylon could not have been involved in the crime. What led you to that conclusion?"

"Well, I must be specific. Our analysis didn't conclude that he didn't commit the crime. The media interpreted it that way. Our tests, though, did show that the physical evidence, especially the DNA, found at the scene, was not related to Henry Waylon."

This was sounding interesting. "Just how did you come to that conclusion?" I asked.

"Because all of the DNA was from a single individual, a male of northern European ancestry. In other words, the DNA at the scene was from a white male, not from an African-American."

Bingo!

"One more question, Ms. Nugent. Do you happen to know the chain of custody of the evidence in question?"

"Yes, as a matter of fact," she said. "It was annotated on the report we got when we received the evidence. It was collected at the scene the morning the body was found, sent to the crime lab, and then returned to the evidence locker, all in a matter of ten days."

So, the crime lab had placed a white male at the scene within ten days of the crime, and months before the trial. There was no way Macauley hadn't known of it, and a good chance that Bavan knew as well. The fuckers had railroaded an innocent man. Sent him to his death, knowing that he was innocent, or at least knowing that there was a reasonable doubt, had the defense had access to that crucial bit of evidence. I had one more question.

"Ms. Nugent, did the police ever identify the person to whom this DNA belonged?"

"No, not as far as I know. You must remember, though, the use of DNA was still rather rudimentary back then. Unless they happened to have a suspect in mind from whom to take a sample for comparison, it's unlikely they'd be able to pinpoint a specific person."

I just happened to have a suspect in mind, and at that point I would have liked to personally rip off a piece of his flesh for comparison. Of course, as an officer of the court, and not wanting to have my license yanked, I wouldn't do that.

I would have to be more subtle.

I thanked Ms. Nugent for her help and rang off.

THIRTY-THREE

I got lucky and found a parking place right in front of Witch's Brew. There were three customers, students from nearby Howard University, sitting together at a table near the counter having coffee, and an elderly woman at the nearest reading table in the middle aisle, hunched over a book. Penelope Payton, wearing a red kerchief on her head and a pink peasant blouse, stood behind the coffee shop counter.

She smiled as I approached the counter.

"Well, the intrepid detective back again," she said. "Did you like the coffee?"

"The coffee was great, but I'm back for more information. Do you have time to talk?"

She looked around the room. The people at the tables were engaged in conversation, and their mugs appeared to be near full. The old woman at the reading table was more engrossed in the book she was reading than her coffee.

"I think I could spare a few minutes," she

said.

She turned to the shelf behind the counter and filled two of the white mugs. Carrying them carefully, she came around the counter and led me to the table nearest the entrance. She sat in the chair that had its back to the door. I sat opposite her, moving my chair so that I could see the three students and the old women, while still engaging her. She pushed one of the mugs toward me.

"Okay, what is it that you want to talk about?" she asked.

I took a sip of coffee. The flavor was strong, with a hint of something sweet. I then put the cup down and looked at her. Her hair was tied back, exposing her ears beneath the scarf, falling down across her back. There was a questioning look in her eyes.

"First, I'll assume that you've heard that Charles Armstrong, one of Way-, er, Henry's roommates, is dead?"

She looked sadly down at her cup. "Yeah, news travels fast down here. Word on the street is it was a heart attack."

So, it seemed that the cops were keeping a lid on it. I could understand that. Until they knew more, they wouldn't to alert the potential suspects. But, I needed to know for myself, and my methods aren't the same as the police. In this case, I felt the best way was to approach it head-on.

"That's probably what the cops want everyone to think," I said. "But, I know in fact that it wasn't. Well, it *was* a heart attack, but it was induced."

Several emotions flashed across her face: shock, confusion, and sadness.

"How do you induce—oh, yes, I seem to remember reading in one of the books I sell here, it can be done by giving heart attach medicine like digitalis to an otherwise healthy person. Is that how it was done to him?"

"I haven't been given the results of the medical examiner's report, but that would be my guess."

Her head turned slowly, and she looked at the plants behind the glass atop the shelves at the back. Her face turned pale.

"Oh, my God," she said.

"What is it?" I asked.

She pointed at the plants.

"Do you know what those plants are?"

I did, but I decided to play dumb.

"They're just flowers to me."

There was a tremor in her voice as she spoke. "Those are foxglove," she said. "They're beautiful flowers, and a lot of people like to intersperse them with other plants in their gardens." She took a deep breath. "They are, however, extremely toxic, which is why I keep them behind glass. Even contact with the leaves and stems can be dangerous."

"Why on earth would anyone want to keep such a plant around?" I continued my dumb act.

"Look at them. They are beautiful. Even knowing their dangers, I like having them here to brighten the place up. But, that's not what shocks me." She sighed, and her shoulders sagged forward. "When you were here before, you asked about Henry's roommates, remember?"

I nodded. I had a nagging sense that I knew what she'd say next.

"Well, I haven't had much contact with

either Chuck or Mike since . . . we were in school together," she said. "But, about two weeks ago, Mike dropped in out of the blue. He said he and Chuck were working in one of the free clinics, and he'd heard that I was running this shop, so he just wanted to drop in and say hello."

"That doesn't seem too unusual."

"No, I suppose not, but it didn't really seem in character for Mike. Chuck, maybe, but Mike was never what I'd call a people person, so needless to say, I was surprised."

"So, what happened?"

She took another sip of coffee. I noticed that her hands were shaking. I was tempted to press her, but letting her get it out at her own pace.

"Not much at first. He just sort of . . . you know . . . talked about old times, what our old classmates were up to, all that is except Henry. He never once mentioned his name, although, I could tell he wanted to." She twisted the coffee mug around on the table, making a low whispering sound as it ground against the surface. "Then, he wanted to see the shop. So, I gave him the ten-cent tour. That's when it really got weird. When I showed him the foxglove, he recognized it, and got really interested. Wanted to know all about it, you know, like where to get plants, stuff like that. I told him you can get seeds or seedlings at some specialty garden shops, and even order some online, but I'd gotten mine from a friend in North Carolina during a visit there. Then, when we walked through the books, he asked if I had any books on foxglove. It turns out I had two, *Medicinal Plants of North America: a Field Guide* and

Plants for a Medieval Garden in the British Isles. Both books have only brief sections on foxglove, but he bought them anyway."

Now, we were getting somewhere.

"Why do you think he was so interested in this plant?"

Her eyes had a haunted look.

"The heart medicine digitalis can be extracted from the foxglove, and if you give digitalis to a healthy person, or a person with a heart condition who is already taking it, you can induce a heart attack. If not treated right away, and I mean right away, that person can die."

Thank you, I thought. If she was the killer, I couldn't see her sitting there describing her method to me. Besides, she looked too stricken.

"Do you think Fletcher's capable of killing someone?"

She stared across the room, looking at something only she could see.

"I've always thought him a bit strange," she said. "But, that day, he really creeped me out."

"Would he have any reason for killing Charles Armstrong? After all, they were friends and work colleagues."

"No, I mean, I don't know. But, if Chuck died from digitalis poison, someone had to have given it to him."

She didn't have to say what she was thinking. I believe we were both thinking the same thing. The look in her eyes said it all. She was scared.

THIRTY-FOUR

Convinced now that Penelope wasn't the killer—more convinced than ever that Michael Fletcher was—I had to worry about what he would do next. The murder of Charles Armstrong worried me. I would have expected Fletcher to go after Bavan, or even the judge, but his murder of someone who didn't fit the victim profile I'd mentally constructed pointed to an entirely different scenario. I now had to consider that Penelope Payton and Yolanda Waylon might very well be targets.

When I pointed this fact out, Penelope's face went even more ashen. She alone lived above her shop, making her easy prey. I couldn't just leave her undefended. Then, I had an idea that I bounced off her.

"How well do you know Henry's sister, Yolanda?" I asked.

"Not very well," she said. "I only met her a couple of times when Henry and I were dating, and I got the distinct impression that she didn't like me very much."

"Well, I have an idea that I think will

benefit the both of you. Let me make a call."

I dialed the MedGen number, only to be told that Yolanda had the day off, but that if I left a number, it would be relayed and if she chose to do so, she could call me back. I asked the nasally voiced woman on the phone to stress to Yolanda that it was urgent.

While I waited, I enjoyed my coffee. Penelope sat mute, staring into her cup.

Yolanda called back in five minutes. When I explained the situation to her, she agreed without hesitation that Penelope should stay with her. She gave us an address on Pierce Street near North Capitol and said she'd be expecting us.

It didn't take much persuading to get Penelope to shoo the customers out and put a closed sign on the door. I then waited while she went upstairs and packed a small suitcase.

The drive south to Yolanda's place, a small two-story brownstone with large vases of stunted evergreens flanking the door, and lacy white curtains on the windows, only took ten minutes, and five of those were spent finding a place to park.

Penelope had sat quietly during the drive, and now, with me carrying her suitcase as we walked toward the steps leading up to the front door, she lagged a bit behind me. I looked back, and could see the apprehensive look on her face.

I walked up the steps, but before I could press the brass doorbell button, the door swung inward.

Yolanda Waylon was wearing cutoff jeans that hugged her dark brown thighs, and an old tee-shirt with no bra—and, in truth, she didn't need one. She smiled at me, and then tilted her head to look at Penelope Payton, who stood two steps behind me looking like a deer caught in the headlights of an oncoming 18-wheeler.

"Why don't y'all come on in," Yolanda said, stepping aside to let me enter.

Penelope came up slowly. She hesitated a couple of heartbeats before crossing the threshold.

"I think you two already know each other," I said.

Yolanda nodded; her face devoid of expression. I turned to Penelope, who still looked like she wanted to turn tail and head for the nearest shelter. Finally, she straightened her shoulders and smiled shyly at Yolanda.

"You look a lot like Henry, you know," she said in a small voice.

Yolanda's lips curled down into a snarl.

"You callin' me ugly?"

Penelope's face turned a nice shade of crimson. She looked like she was about to burst into tears.

"N-no, I was definitely n-not. You're a very attractive w-woman. You know, p-people used to say that Henry was too g-good looking to be a man, anyway."

Yolanda held the snarl on her face for a long time, her eyes blazing for what I took to be anger. I was just preparing to step between them, when she suddenly doubled over, clutching her stomach, and . . . laughing.

I'm not sure who looked more astonished, me or Penelope. Finally, Yolanda stood, wiping tears from her liquid brown eyes.

"Aw, girl, don't look so stricken," she said. "I was just yanking your chain." She took the four steps to cross the space separating them and held out her hand. "Welcome to my house. I should be a bit pissed at you, you know. All this time you been running a business this close to where I live, and you never once came to visit me."

Penelope's face was still flushed, and her cheeks glistened where tears had flowed over them. She took Yolanda's brown hand in her pale one.

"I've wanted to, but, I always thought you didn't care much for me. Besides, you have your family."

"Well, you know, I didn't like you too much back then," Yolanda said. "But, you gotta remember, I was just fifteen, and you were stealing my big brother away from me. I've grown up since then, and hope a bit wiser. As for family, mama died while I was in the army. Henry was the only family I had left." Now, her cheeks showed tear tracks.

"He was all I had left as well."

"I guess that makes us both orphans," Yolanda said. "Not a bad way to start a friendship."

"We have that in common, and one other thing," Penelope said. "We both loved Henry very much."

They embraced then. Like long lost sisters—which in a way they were—sisters bonded together by mutual love and mutual loss. I'd done my part, now I had another job to do.

"You two look out for each other," I said, as I headed for the door.

THIRTY-FIVE

By the time I got back to my car, it was getting on to 4:30. I had one more thing to do before the weekend. I was planning on going fishing, and I had just enough time to set the bait.

A fender bender involving a mini-van and a garbage truck four blocks from Yolanda's house caught me in the middle of the block behind stalled traffic. The garbage truck had skidded and was blocking both lanes of traffic, and the dumb shit behind me was following so close, I couldn't back up. When I thought the two harried looking cops trying to make sense out of the mess weren't looking, I turned my steering wheel sharp left, and did an illegal U-turn.

It took me a few minutes to figure out which cross street to take to get back in the direction of the free clinic. DC's like that. So many streets just come to an abrupt end at a cross street, or diagonally crossing avenue, it you don't know the layout of a neighborhood, you can drive around for a while trying to figure your way out of an area. When Pierre Charles L'Enfant and Benjamin Banneker laid out the capital city in the late 1700s, what had been envisioned was a grand city of wide avenues, public squares and magnificent buildings symbolizing the equality of all men. Over two hundred years later, the hand of man—especially the politicians who have run the city, some would say into the ground—has converted all but the impressive National Mall downtown into a warren of one-way streets, half streets, cul-de-sacs, and diagonal avenues. Washington, DC is the only city I've ever been in where you can take four right turns and not end up near your starting point. In fact, do that in the wrong part of town, and you can become hopelessly lost.

All that meant was that a journey that should have taken me ten minutes turned into a forty minute ordeal, and when I arrived in the area of the clinic, I still had the task of finding a place to park. By the time I walked into the clinic reception area, it was 5:50, and the only person there was the woman at the desk.

She smiled broadly as I entered.

"You again," she said. "You keep this up, and we're gonna have to give you a discount card."

I smiled at her lame attempt at humor. After my drive, I wasn't in the mood to do more.

"Is Dr. Fletcher still here?" I asked.

"You're in luck. He hasn't left yet. I'll call back and let him know you're here."

I knew the drill. Have a seat, and he'll be

right out. I took my now accustomed seat at the back row, while she picked up the phone and muttered something unintelligible into it.

At 6:05, Fletcher came into the room His scrubs were still immaculate. I wondered how he managed it. Even the receptionist had a few wrinkles and stains. His looked like he'd just taken them off the ironing board. He even had creases in his pants. He still had that blank look on his face.

"What can I do for you?" he asked. If voices had looks, his voice would have been a blank look.

"I heard about your friend, Charles Armstrong," I said. "My condolences."

He stood there, about four feet away, his hands shoved into the pockets of his scrubs, with his head cocked to one side.

"Yeah, tough about that. Man, you just never know when the old ticker's gonna pop. Chuck was a good friend."

For all the emotion in his voice he could have been reading the prices from a supermarket ad. I could see how he'd freaked Penelope out. Hell, he was beginning to get to me.

"You know," I said. "His death wasn't from natural causes—or whatever it is you doctors say to indicate a person not dying by the agency of some external force."

"Huh?" He looked at me with an expression of total incomprehension.

"I mean, he was murdered. Someone introduced some substance into his body that caused his heart to stop working."

There was the first flicker of something in those dead eyes of his—tiny, but there nonetheless.

Now, the flicker was more than just momentary. The muscles of his face were still except for a barely discernible twitch under his right eye. But, his eyes were suddenly seeing me. There was something there, and it didn't look good.

"Chuck was . . . murdered? Who in hell would want to kill a harmless little mouse like Charles Armstrong?"

Time to throw out the first piece of bait. "I've been thinking that same thing myself," I said. "I mean, the only way I could see him being a threat enough to someone that they'd want to kill him is maybe he knew something his killer didn't want him to reveal."

He sat down in the chair in front of me, with his legs thrust out to the side. He looked at the point of my chin rather than into my eyes.

"What could he possibly know that would be a threat to anyone?"

He tried to keep his voice level, but I could detect a little tension in it, and the way he leaned toward me as he spoke also indicated the tension he was feeling. I decided to give him a little more bait.

"That's what I'm determined to find out. There's another thing—do you remember the prosecutor in Henry Waylon's case; Thomas Macauley?"

He clenched his lips and scrunched up his forehead, but it didn't fool me. There's no way he could have forgotten.

"Oh yeah, I remember him," he said. "A distasteful little man."

"Well, someone did him in the same way they did your friend. I'm convinced it was the same person."

"So, what are you going to do about it?" He had a querying look in his face, but I heard the challenge in his voice.

Now was the time to set the bait and get ready to reel the sucker in.

"I intend to find him and put him where he belongs—behind bars for the rest of his stinking life."

I saw the brief blaze of anger in his eyes. His jaws clenched so tight, the muscles in his cheeks quivered. But, he was good. He said nothing for a moment. Just sat there looking at me. Then, he stood and jammed his hands in his pockets.

"How are you even going to know where to start?"

"Oh, I already have a start," I said. "First, there's the similarities between the two murders, and the unique way they were committed. I'm convinced the two killings were not only related to each other, but to the Waylon case."

He was staring at me intently now.

"I think there was something a bit hinky about that whole trial," I continued. "And, tomorrow I'm talking to someone who can clear that up for me."

His body leaned forward slightly. I could tell that I really had his interest now.

"Really, who would that be after all these years?"

"The cop who headed the investigation," I said. "You remember him, don't you, a detective named Allan Bavan? He's retired now, and living on a houseboat over near the waterfront. He called and asked to talk to me tomorrow afternoon. Said he had some information that would blow the Macauley killing wide open, and would clear up a wrong that was done ten years ago. I don't know exactly what he meant, but my bet is it'll put me closer to identifying the person who killed Macauley *and* your friend."

"Well, good luck with that," he said.

Small beads of sweat had popped out on his forehead, and as hard as he tried to look unconcerned, I could see a flicker of worry on his face; a slight reddening of the cheeks and a little tic below his left eye. But, he was still a cool customer.

"I've gotta go now," he said. "It's been a long day."

He turned, and walked away.

Putting this son of a bitch away was going to be a pleasure.

THIRTY-SIX

I left the clinic and drove home. Sandra was waiting, dressed to go out to dinner. When I told her I'd have to take a raincheck, her face fell. She wasn't any happier when I told her why.

"You're taking an awful chance, you know," she said. "And, you're using this man Bavan for bait? What does he have to say about that?"

"Uh, well . . . the thing is, I haven't told him yet."

She took a step back and stared at me, her mouth agape.

"Al Pennyback, you set this up without even getting his consent? I can't believe you'd do a thing like that."

Okay, so she doesn't know me as well as she thought.

"If I'd asked him he might have turned me down," I said. "This way, he'll have no choice but to go along."

"And, you see nothing wrong with that?"

I shrugged. "If you knew this guy the way I know him, you'd agree with me that this is the only way to handle this situation."

"I'll fix you a couple of sandwiches and a thermos of coffee," she said. She was shaking her head as she headed for the kitchen.

It's not that my moral compass is broken. Even though I had no great love for Allan Bavan—no love at all for that matter—I wouldn't allow him to be killed. If my plan worked the way I envisioned it, he would only be in moderate danger, and he was a trained cop, so he ought to be able to deal with moderate danger. Or so my reasoning went.

While Sandra prepared my stakeout meal, I went to my bedroom and started getting into my night operation gear. Black cargo pants, the kind with pockets on each leg; black mesh tee-shirt, black nylon jacket—even in summer, it can get chilly late at night—black canvas boots, and a black skull cap made from nylon and with a pull-down flap that covered my face and cupped under my chin, allowing me to melt into the darkness without suffocating.

Despite what they show in all the movies and TV shows about private detectives, I never carry a gun. I qualify on the range every year just to keep my license current, but I neither own nor carry a sidearm. I had enough of guns in the army, and decided that if I found in myself in a situation that I couldn't talk my way out of, or fight my way out of with hands and feet—I have fourth-degree black belts in Taekwondo and Karate—I would just run away. One of my Korean Taekwondo instructors was fond of telling me that there's no shame in running away, if it allowed you to live to fight another day. I did, however, carry a K-bar knife, in a sheath strapped to my right ankle, only for dire situations.

When I came back to the living room, Sandra was waiting with a brown paper bag and a one-quart thermos, which she handed me. She was frowning, but she leaned in and gave me a sisterly peck on the cheek.

"I'm still a bit upset with you," she said. "But, I guess I can understand why you're doing things this way."

"Trust me, this is the best way—well, the best I could come up with given the time and circumstances."

She kissed me again. "Just be careful."

"Always am."

It was nearly 9:00 when I parked on Water Street, about two blocks from Bavan's houseboat. It was just beginning to get dark. Full dark in late July isn't until 9:30 or a few minutes after. I began making my way to the boat.

At that hour on Friday night, there were lots of people in the waterfront area, but luckily for me, most of them were at the north end of Water Street where the seafood restaurants are. I nonetheless stayed as much in the shadows as possible, keeping to the land side of the street instead of the water side where I would have stood out like a scarecrow in the middle of a newly harvested field.

I didn't figure Fletcher would have made his move yet. He would want to wait until there was no one around, which meant well after midnight in this area. That, I thought, would give me ample time to convince Bavan to go along with my plan and find a place to conceal myself to wait.

Bavan was in his usual place, sitting on a chair at the stern of his boat, with a half-empty bottle of whiskey on the table, and a large water glass full of whiskey in his hand. None of the boat lights were on, but the nearby street lamp provided enough illumination to see him sprawled in the chair, his grimy tee-shirt riding high on his gut, and his double chins resting on his chest.

At first I thought he was asleep, but when I stepped onto the gangplank, he lifted his head and his glass.

"Hey, if it ain't my favor-right private eye," he said. His voice wasn't as slurred as it had been the last time I visited. He must have just started his evening drinking. "To what do I owe the pleasure of thish visit?"

I sat in the empty chair across from him, glad that the evening breeze seemed to be coming from my rear. Even so, the pungent odor of his unwashed body was making my nose itch.

I told him why I'd come.

He put his glass on the table and leaned forward. In the dim light from the street lamp, I could see the anger—and fear—in his bloodshot eyes.

"Are you fucking insane?" he said. "You paint a fucking target on my back to bait a freako killer, and you don't even have the fucking decency to ask me first?"

He didn't get up and try to punch me, so that was a plus. On the other hand, he might've just been too drunk to stand up.

"Look, I know I should have talked to you first, but things happened so fast. I saw an opportunity, and I had to take it. You're a cop, you know how it is. You have to make a split decision so a perp doesn't walk free."

He slouched back, still glaring up at me, but blinking his eyes as if he was having difficulty focusing.

"Yeah," he said finally. "I guess I can see that. I've had to make a few decisions like that myself. 'Sides, I remember that punk, Fletcher. He was sort of a smart ass. Hadn't been for his buddy, Armstrong giving him an alibi, I might've looked at him as a possible suspect."

That caught my attention.

"Armstrong gave him an alibi?"

"Well, yeah . . . sort of," he said. He scratched his head, his fingers making a rasping sound on his bald pate. "I mean, Armstrong said they were in the bar when Waylon left, and I . . . shit, I guess I just assumed he meant they were together the whole time."

It took a few seconds for it to penetrate his booze-addled brain.

"Oh shit," he said. "That means-"

"That you focused on Henry Waylon, while the real killer walked right from under your nose," I finished for him.

He slumped, resting his hands on his knees.

"Shit. Then, Macauley's stunt with the trace evidence put the wrong man away," he said. "Aw, shit!"

"You knew that Macauley withheld evidence from the defense?"

He finally looked up at me. There was a haunted look in his eyes.

"Yeah, I knew. He did shit like that a lot.

Winning was all that counted for that fucker. Most times, it didn't matter, but . . . that kid, Waylon . . . well, he wasn't like some of the other gangbangers I ran in. He seemed like a decent kid, but he refused to account for his whereabouts or movements when he left the bar, so . . ."

"So, you made an assumption. Did it ever occur to you that he might have been drugged, and that was why he didn't remember anything?"

"Drugged—you mean like a ruffie? Naw, I didn't. Date rape drugs back then were used primarily on women. I didn't think about them being used on a dude. You think he was drugged?"

I described the inconsistency in the trial transcript between Fletcher and Armstrong's accounts of the moments before Waylon complained about being dizzy.

"They were med students," he said. "Maybe Fletcher had access to the drugs."

"Or knew how to make them," I said. "Med students take chemistry, you know."

He leaned forward, his elbows on his knees, and his head cupped in his hands.

"Man, I really fucked it up on that one, didn't I," he said in a muffled voice.

"Yeah, but now, though, you have a chance to make up for it in a small way," I said.

He looked up. Some of the old cop fire was back in his eyes.

"Okay, what do you want me to do?"

THIRTY-SEVEN

Buster, and most of the cops I've ever spoken to, hate stakeouts. After three hours sitting on a folding chair Bavan had taken from his houseboat's galley, I had nothing but sympathy for them. I'd long since eaten the two tuna salad sandwiches Sandra made for me, along with half the coffee. As tempting as it was, though, I held off on drinking too much. It would be just my luck to be taking a leak when Fletcher arrived. Even without the urge to pee, my muscles were stiffening from sitting in one place so long. I'd at least been lucky enough to find a place with solid soil, behind a begonia bush that was tall enough to conceal me, but with enough space among the leaves to give me clear line of sight on the houseboat.

Bavan had finally gone along with my plan, but he warned me just as I was leaving his boat that if Fletcher got past me and killed me he'd come back to haunt the hell out of me for the rest of my life. I don't believe in ghosts—well, I'm not sure if ghosts exist or not—but, since I'd come up with the plan, I felt that I had a responsibility to keep him alive.

The plan was pure simplicity. I would wait in the bushes until Fletcher came skulking up with the aim of silencing Bavan. I was figuring he would, like most killers, stick to the same M.O., and find a way to introduce his heart-attack-inducing toxin into the fat man's system. To make it easier, I'd convinced Bavan to leave the half-empty whiskey bottle on the table. That, along with the stained glass, would make it look like the man was a boozer, which was accurate. Caught with the poison in his possession, he'd have a hard time convincing anyone he didn't kill the other two men.

The late night dinner crowd, mostly tourists doing the summer vacation in the Nation's Capital bit, thinned out around ten, and was entirely gone by midnight. The waiters and clean-up crews were an hour behind them, leaving the night to predators and hunters. I was a hunter waiting for a predator.

Bavan had gone deeper into the boar around eleven, and I only hoped he'd stayed sober enough to be able to fulfill his part of my plan.

I stole a quick glance at the luminous face of my watch. The soft green numerals showed that it was 1:30, although I could have guessed the time within five or ten minutes, a skill I'd learned in the army. When the glow of a watch face while on patrol could get you killed, you learned to *feel* the passage of time and know what time it was, more or less.

The day had been a scorcher, but by midnight, the heat of the day had burned off. It felt like the temperature had dropped twenty degrees, and while sixty degrees isn't technically cold, after sweating in eighty degree heat, a drop like that can give you a chill. Hypothermia is a real problem. I brought my light jacket, but still shivered in the chilly air.

The quiet, after all the daytime noise of cars and people, felt strange. At my farm, except for the bird calls and the chirping of insects, it's always quiet, so nightfall is only a matter of a change in the light level. Here in the city, though, it was as if someone had turned a switch. The roar of engines and honking of horns had been replaced by the sounds of night creatures that started softly at first, but continued to rise in volume as if the insects had been waiting for their turn.

I was just fighting the temptation to take a sip of coffee from the mug when I felt a change in the tempo and volume of insect sounds off to my right. I put the thermos down softly and, after pulling the mask down over my face, I leaned forward in the chair to get a look down Water Street through the gaps in the foliage.

A man moved toward me, keeping to the shadows. From the general height and size, I was pretty sure it was Fletcher. His stealthy movements and the fact that he darted quickly whenever he came to a pool of light from the weak street lamps only confirmed it.

As he passed through the light from the lamp nearest I got a glimpse of his face. It *was* Fletcher. He was dressed, as I was, in black; black pants and a long sleeved black shirt. In his right hand he carried a small parcel. He looked to right and left as he came abreast of the houseboat. He stood there for a full minute before quickly crossing the street. At the foot of the gangplank, he paused, cocking his head, and then stepped gingerly up the ramp and onto the houseboat's aft deck.

I eased from my hiding place and started making my way toward the houseboat, hoping he wouldn't turn and see me. My worry was groundless. He took out a penlight and waved it around the deck, the pencil-thin beam coming to rest on the whiskey bottle. He put the flashlight in his mouth and knelt next to the table. I couldn't see what he was doing, but he was so intent on whatever it was, I was able to get to the foot of the gangplank unobserved.

When he lifted the whiskey bottle to shake it, I stepped up onto the deck. He put the bottle down and stood.

"Hold it right there," I said.

"Wha-" He whirled around, his eyes wide in shock.

Just then, lights in the overhead came on. I closed my eyes, but not before seeing the flash. I opened my eyes to spots dancing before them, which took a second or two to resolve into Fletcher standing there, swaying from side to side with his hand over his eyes.

"Wha-" he said again.

"Get your fucking hands up, turkey," Bavan said.

He stood in the doorway, a 9mm Sig Sauer in his right hand pointed at Fletcher.

"Get down on your knees and put your hands on top of your head," he said.

Fletcher turned sideways, his head swiveling right to left and back again like a spectator at a table tennis match. He moved his left hand toward the whiskey bottle. Bavan raised the automatic and pointed it at his head.

"Touch that bottle and I'll blow your head off," he said.

Fletcher froze, bent slightly forward with his left hand hovering over the bottle.

"If I were you, I'd do what he says," I said softly. "The way his hand's shaking, he's just apt to shoot you by accident."

I pulled the skullcap off. The night air felt good on my face.

A trapped animal, despite facing insurmountable odds, will sometimes fight. At other times, though, the rational brain kicks in, and the trapped animal, realizing that the end is inevitable, simply, meekly accepts its fate. Fletcher's eyes darted from side to side. Part of him wanted to make a break for it. Fortunately for him his rational brain took over.

He raised his hands, placing them on top of his head, and dropped to his knees.

I moved forward and picked up the little package he'd put on the floor while he doctored Bavan's whiskey. It was a little black travel bag with a Velcro fastener, like the kind they give business class passengers on international flights. I could feel the shape of two cylindrical objects through the fabric—he'd come loaded for bear.

"Move over toward the corner," I told Fletcher. He hastily complied, scooting over on his knees.

I didn't want him tempted to try and

destroy the whiskey bottle, which I was sure contained the contents of at least one of the cylindrical objects I'd felt in the travel kit. That was an important piece of evidence.

Bavan stood there, looking almost as befuddled as Fletcher. The Sig was now mercifully pointing at the deck. I saw that his hand shook a little, whether from all the booze he'd drunk or from nerves, I couldn't tell, but I was glad it hadn't come to a shootout. In his condition, he was as likely to have hit me as Fletcher.

"Man," he said quietly. "We did it. We caught him."

"Yeah, we caught him," I said, as I took out my mobile phone and dialed 911.

THIRTY-EIGHT

Three weeks later, on August 16, I found myself sitting in Mom's on Sixteenth Street waiting for Buster.

He'd called and invited me to have lunch, an unusual occurrence. And, even more unusual, he was late.

I was sitting at our usual table, in the right corner, with my back to the wall so I could see outside through the picture window, while at the same time keeping an eye on the inside, which at the moment was somewhat crowded with a mélange of blacks and Hispanics, mostly male, and mostly dressed in the overalls and reflective vests of DC road crews, when Mom, a mountain of a woman, walked into my field of view.

Calling Mom huge is like calling water wet—so obvious. The woman weighs at least 300 pounds. Today she was dressed in a blue dress with white polka dots that contained enough fabric to do two tents of a three-ring circus. Her hair was jet black, and shiny, and hot ironed to a fare the well. It stuck to her head like it had been glued in place. Mom is ageless. She's been the proprietor of DC's best soul food joint forever, and even though the place has gone through a number of name changes over the years, the menu, I'm told is the same as it was in the late sixties. For reasons I've never understood, Mom has taken a liking to Buster and me, treating us like misbehaving sons some time. Like, for instance, she never gives us a menu. Instead, she tells us to sit down and she'll 'fix something up for us.' The food is always so good, though, we never complain.

"Where that no good friend of yours?" she asked.

I looked up at her smiling face.

"I don't know," I said. "It's not like him to be late."

"Well, if he don't hurry up, I'm gone serve your meal, and he ain't gone git nothin'."

"It would serve him right. Can I have another cup of that fine coffee of yours, please?"

Her smile got wider and she reached over and patted my shoulder. I'm her favorite, because I'm such a gentleman.

"Sure enough, hon," she said. As she turned to get my coffee, she spoke over her shoulder, "I sure wish some of your manners would rub off on that Buster."

At that moment, the ringing of the bell over the door, announced Buster's arrival. He stopped just inside the door, and eyed Mom and me with narrowed eyes.

"You two been talking about me, haven't you?"

Mom patted his dark brown, chiseled

cheeks.

"Now, why on earth would we be wantin' to talk 'bout you, child? Gone and set down, so I can git you some lunch made."

He sat across from me, and put a thick brown envelope on the table.

"Sorry to keep you waiting, bro," he said. "But, just as I was leavin' the captain called me into his office."

I took a sip of coffee.

"No problem, I've just been sitting here enjoying Mom's coffee. What's up? It's usually me inviting you to lunch."

He patted the envelope.

"I was coming to tell you what's happened since you nabbed that bastard, Fletcher. Figured you had a right to know. Oh, and by the way, that was a nice piece Lucy Mendez did about you in the Sunday *Post*. The Brown Knight sees justice done again. That gall really likes you, you know."

I shrugged. I've long since become mostly immune to the stories Lucy writes. I *did* want to know more about the case, however, but I'd never make an issue of it. Besides, I can always get Heather to ferret it out of one of her contacts or off the Internet for me. I'd never tell Buster that, though.

"Yeah, it'd be nice to know my efforts were appreciated."

"Well, the captain wasn't too pleased at first—neither was the chief for that matter. They felt a civilian had no business pulling a dangerous operation like that."

I looked at him with raised brows. He held his hands up in a gesture of supplication.

"Hey, I'm just tellin' you what they said.

I kept my mouth shut. I know you're tougher than any ten cops, but they don't need to know that. Anyway, it worked, and they can stand up in front of the press and claim the credit. That's not the point, though. The point is, after we sweated the dude for a while, he finally cracked and confessed to killing both Armstrong and Macauley."

"I was right about it. That's good to know."

"Yeah, but that ain't all."

He snapped his mouth shut and looked at me, grinning.

"Okay," I said. "I'll bite. What else is there?"

"I know you don't watch TV, and probably don't pay too much attention to the news, but did you hear about two old dudes over in Virginia dying from heart attacks last month—two men who happened to have served on the jury that convicted Henry Waylon?"

It took me a moment, but I did recall Heather pointing them out to me.

"Yeah, but what does that have to do with—wait, are you telling me those men were also murdered?"

"Like I said, Fletcher cracked, cracked wide open," he said. "He also confessed to raping and killing Colleen Adamson in 1992. It seems he was irritated that Adamson was coming on to Waylon and not him, so he slipped some Special K, that's ketamine, into their drinks. Then, when the girl got dizzy, and went outside, he followed her. That shit can really mess up a person's mind, and he got her down by Key Bridge, but he must have messed up on the amount he gave her, 'cause she started coming out from under while he was raping her, so he strangled her and hid her under the bridge."

"So, when Henry Waylon claimed he didn't remember anything, he was telling the truth."

"Yeah, ketamine causes short term memory loss," he said. "It don't stay in the system too long, and the fucking cops over cross the river never tested him for drugs anyway."

No wonder Bavan had looked so stricken when I dropped the news on him that Michael Fletcher was the likely killer.

"But, what does this have to with the two jurors?"

"Oh, yeah, that's the weird part. That asshole Fletcher was testing dosages. He didn't want a repeat of what happened with Adamson. So, he mixed up doses of digitalis he made from boiling leaves from-" He opened the envelope and pulled out several sheets of paper. He flipped through until he found the one he was looking for. "Yeah, here it is. Foxglove. He bought some foxglove plants and was keeping them in his apartment. When he was ready to kill someone, he'd brew up some more juice. In Macauley's case, he met him when he was out jogging, and offered him a drink of this special tea he said would help his stamina. He killed his friend Armstrong by slipping some into drinks they were having at Armstrong's place."

"How the hell did he get to the two old men? Surely they wouldn't take anything to drink from a total stranger."

"He wasn't a stranger," Buster said. "The

son of a bitch volunteered his services at the old folk's home where one of the old men lived, and at several senior centers around the area. He's a doctor, remember. They had no reason not to trust him. And, get this, he picked them at random to test the dosages it'd need to kill a man, like he was doing some kinda high school science experiment. He kept notes and everything."

I could feel that anger at Fletcher coming back. Before I could say anything, though, Mom came back carrying a large tray, which she sat on the edge of the table. It was laden with two large dinner plates, two medium sized saucers and a pitcher. The plates were filled to overflowing with breaded pork chops, collard greens, and candied yams. Each saucer held two large golden brown cornbread muffins, and the pitcher contained ice tea. Mom put a plate and saucer in front of each of us, and then filled two glasses with tea. Buster emptied three sugar containers into his and began to stir it. I prefer mine unsweetened, which Mom thinks is sacrilege. As a southerner, she likes her tea so sweet you can see the sugar crystals barely dissolved as they reflect light.

When she'd arranged everything to her satisfaction, she stood back and beamed down at us.

"Okay, boys, eat up," she said. "I wants to see them plates clean when I come back with dessert."

"Dessert," I said. "Mom, you have to be kidding. If we eat all this, there won't be room for anything else."

"Aw, pish, hon, they's always room for dessert. I think you'll like my special dessert, too. It's blackberry pie with a scoop of vanilla ice cream on top."

"Shut up, bro," Buster said, already beginning to dig into his food. "Mom knows what she's talking about."

I know when I'm outvoted, and the thought of blackberry pie was making my mouth water, as were the aromas wafting from the plate in front of me.

"Yes, ma'am<" I said. "My plate will be clean."

She laughed and waddled off. For a few minutes, we ate in silence.

The food was good, but there was still something nagging at me. Finally, I put my fork down and placed my elbows on the table.

"I wouldn't do that if I was you," Buster said. "You know how Mom is 'bout eating with your elbows on the table."

"I'm not eating now," I said. "I'm just wondering something. Macauley had to know Waylon was innocent. The DNA was from a white guy, yet he prosecuted him anyway. It makes no sense."

Buster's face contorted in anger, and he put his fork down.

"Of course that son of a bitch knew Waylon was innocent. But, they couldn't get any identification on the DNA, and feelings over there were pretty high. Besides, Macauley liked to win, and he had a pretty good circumstantial case against Waylon, so he went for it. Hell, what'd he care? Waylon was just some black kid."

"How do people like that live with themselves, and how did the DA's office let him get away with it?"

"Hey, everybody likes a winner. But, in

Macauley's case, it got so bad, they asked him to resign. That's why he wound up working for a defense lobbying firm. He left the DA's office and they kept quiet about his past."

"I'm not saying I'm sorry the bastard's dead, but why did Fletcher kill him—or Armstrong either for that matter?"

"Fletcher's a doctor. He keeps up with what's happening in science and all that shit. He knew that if the case ever got looked at, there was a likelihood the cops would ask for a sample of his and Armstrong's DNA, and he'd be fried. Then, he found out that Armstrong had asked the Innocence Project to look into it, so he figured he'd have to go. He did Macauley to make it look like someone was getting revenge for Waylon's execution. He also sent the threatening note to Judge Carson as part of his plan. If you hadn't been digging into that threat, he might've gotten away with it, too."

Not that any of this would bring Henry Waylon back, but there was a tiny bit of satisfaction in seeing the scales of justice almost in balance.

"Speaking of Judge Carson," I said. "Did you hear he withdrew his name from consideration as a federal judge, and submitted his retirement?"

"Yeah, too bad in a way. He was a hard ass, but he followed the law. If he'd known what Macauley was doing, I think he'd of smashed his nuts."

I didn't respond to that. I found it hard to believe that a judge of Carson's intelligence and experience had no clue that a prosecutor who regularly appeared before him was playing fast and loose with the rules. My own feeling was that Carson had, like Macauley, become a captive to the system, a system that was more concerned with the appearance of law and order, of showing people that you're tough on crime, than getting true justice. It didn't help that he was a black man working in a system that placed less value on the lives of people of color than the majority. A system that tended not to look beyond the surface condition of skin color. Maybe I was being too harsh in my judgment of the man, but I was relieved when I delivered my final report to him that there was no threat. He thanked me and gave me a check for the days I'd worked, throwing in an extra thousand as a bonus. I thanked him, and got off his property as fast as the Volkswagen would take me without going into a skid. When the news reported his retirement the following day, I ignored it.

"Maybe you're right," I said. "But, the good judge could have shown a bit more compassion. Justice has to be about more than just a set of rules."

"Hey, I know how you feel about the death penalty, man, but as bad as the law is sometimes, think about what it would be like without it. Oh, another thing, since Fletcher killed three people in Virginia, well, four counting Adamson, and only one here in the District, our city attorney has agreed to let Virginia try him first."

I was just lifting a fork of yams from my plate. My hand stopped halfway to my mouth.

"Would that be because Virginia has the death penalty and the District doesn't?"

"Precisely." He nodded. "Look, I know how you feel. Sometimes, I'm not so sure myself whether the death penalty makes sense. I ain't seen no proof that it keeps people from killing. But, if you look at what Fletcher did—I mean, if there's a dude who deserves to die, it's him."

One part of me agreed with him. What Michael Fletcher had done was beyond inhumane. To so callously kill two old men testing his plans to kill two more was something that I, despite my own experiences in battle, found hard to get my mind around. But, deep down, I still felt that capital punishment was nothing more than official revenge, an eye for an eye, which only leaves everyone blind. Unfortunately, human nature being what it is, there will always be those who see it as justified, just as there will always be people like Thomas Macauley who believe that the ends justifies the means— even if those means themselves are illegal.

I realized, though, that there was nothing I could do to change the system, other than making sure that whenever I came into contact with it I did my best to always try and do the right thing.

"Well, it's out of both our hands now," I said. "We can't change it by worrying about it. Hell, we can't change it at all. We can just do the best we can, when we can."

"Right on, bro," he said. He looked over his shoulder and smiled. Mom was coming out of the kitchen carrying two plates with steaming slices of apple pie and already melting mounds of ice cream. "And, right now, the thing we can do best is eat some of Mom's delicious apple pie."

I breathed in deeply. The sweet smell of apple and cinnamon felt right, and the anticipation of the competing warmth of the pie and the chill of the ice cream gave me hope that, like Mom's apple pie, things would someday come out right.

More adventures of Al Pennyback

Deadly Vendetta

When a bomb intended for a local mobster kills the wife of one of Al's old army buddies, and the law doesn't seem interested, it's up to Al and his friends to see that justice is done.

Death Wish

In the wake of the 9/11 terrorist attacks, there is a lot of money to be made in working for the government. There are some who will do anything to earn a profit, despite the best efforts at oversight. When a young sergeant who notices irregularities goes missing, his commander asks Al to find him.

A Deadly Wind Blows

Al is hired to find a missing heiress and convince her to return to Washington to claim her inheritance. Someone is determined to stop him, even if it means killing him.

See these and other books by this author at: http://www.amazon.com/Charles-Ray/e/B006WMLEZK

Other books by this author:

Al Pennyback mysteries

Color Me Dead
Memorial to the Dead
Deadline
Dead, White, and Blue
A Good Day to Die
The Day the Music Died
Die, Sinner
Deadly Intentions
Death by Design
Till Death Do Us Part
Deadly Dose
Dead Man's Cove
Dead Men Don't Answer
Deadly Paradise
Kiss of Death
Death in White Satin
Death and Taxis
Deadbeat
A Deadly Wind Blows
Death Wish
Deadly Vendetta
A Time to Kill, A Time to Die

The Buffalo Soldier series:

Buffalo Soldier: Trial by Fire
Buffalo Soldier: Homecoming
Buffalo Soldier: Incident at Cactus Junction
Buffalo Soldier: Peacekeepers
Buffalo Soldier: Renegade
Buffalo Soldier: Escort Duty
Buffalo Soldier: Battle at Dead Man's Gulch
Buffalo Soldier: Yosemite
Buffalo Soldier: Comanchero
Buffalo Soldier: Range War
Buffalo Soldier: Mob Justice

Other fiction
Angel on His Shoulder
She's No Angel
Child of the Flame
Pip's Revenge
Wallace in Underland
Further Adventures of Wallace in Underland
Dead Letter and Other Tales
The White Dragons
The Dragon's Lair
Dragon Slayer
The Last Gunfighters
The Culling
Frontier Justice: Bass Reeves, Deputy
  U.S. Marshal
Angel on His Shoulder-Revised Edition

Battle at the Galactic Junkyard

Nonfiction

Things I Learned from My Grandmother About Leadership and Life

Taking Charge: Effective Leadership for the Twenty-first Century

Grab the Brass ring

African Places: A Photographic Journey Through Zimbabwe and southern Africa

A Portrait of Africa

There's Always a Plan B

In the Line of Fire: American Diplomats in the Trenches

Children's books

The Yak and the Yeti

Samantha and the Bully

Molly Learns to Share

Where is Teddy?

Catie and Mister Hop-Hop

About the Author

Charles Ray has been writing fiction since his teens. He won a Sunday school magazine writing contest when he was thirteen, and having his byline on a short story published in a national publication forever hooked him on writing. During his time in the army (1962-1982) he often moonlighted as a newspaper or magazine journalist, and was the editorial cartoonist for the Spring Lake (NC) News, a weekly newspaper, during the 1970s. In addition to his writing, he was an artist/cartoonist and photographer for a number of publications, including Ebony, Eagle and Swan, and Essence, and had a monthly cartoon feature and did several covers for Buffalo, a now-defunct magazine that was dedicated to showcasing the contributions of African-Americans to the country's military history.

After retiring from the army, he joined the U.S. Foreign Service, and served as a diplomat in posts in Asia and Africa until his retirement in 2012. He has worked and traveled throughout the world (Antarctica is the only continent he hasn't visited), and now, as a full time writer, continues to globetrot looking for interesting things to write about, draw, or take pictures of.

A native of Texas, he now calls Maryland

home. For more on his writing and other projects, check one of the following Web sites:

http://charlesaray.blogspot.com
http://charlieray45.wordpress.com
http://www.twitter.com/charlieray45
http://www.facebook.com/charlieray45
http://www.flickr.com/photos/charlesray45/
http://www.viewbug.com/member/charlesray

Author's photograph by Denise Ray-Wickersham

www.ingramcontent.com/pod-product-compliance
Lightning Source LLC
Chambersburg PA
CBHW061947170626
46813CB00006B/2556